183

D0457552

# The Ballad
## of
# Castle Reef

*Honor Tracy*

# The Ballad
# of
# Castle Reef

cop. 2

*Random House*
*New York*

First American Edition

Copyright © 1979 by Honor Tracy

Library of Congress Cataloging in Publication Data

Tracy, Honor Lilbush Wingfield, 1915-
    The ballad of Castle Reef.

    I. Title.
PZ4.T762Bal    1980      [PR6070.R25]      823'.9'14      79-4785
ISBN 0-394-50689-8

Manufactured in the United States of America

9 8 7 6 5 4 3 2

# Chapter One

For generations, centuries indeed, the Barracloughs of Castle Reef had been soldiers. It had never crossed their minds that there was anything else to be. When, therefore, Major Arthur Barraclough, DSO, a few years before this story begins, received a letter from his son and heir to say the life was not for him, he felt as if the sky had fallen.

The Major was the first to admit that the Army had gone to the dogs. You need look no further than a modern recruiting appeal to realise that. Composed by some long-haired PRO, who apparently had learned his craft in America, it read like a puff for a holiday camp. And the FCs, or Floosie Corps, as he ungallantly termed the women's sector, were a permanent thorn in his side.

But the Army had gone to the dogs in his father's day as well, when the famous crowd in which the Barracloughs served was combined, willy nilly, with a rabble of clots. It had done likewise in that of his grandfather, when the cavalry regiments were mechanized and commissions given to bounders. And the process had begun much earlier yet. The family archives we⁀ full of letters and diaries, musty and yellow, grieving over thᵤ milestones along the Army's downward path. There was the pampering initiated by Florence Nightingale, for instance, and the abolition of flogging. An entry in one journal, made on the eve of Waterloo, bemoaned the loss of fighting spirit among the rank and file; and a note in the margin by another hand, endorsing this, placed the turning-point at about the time of Malplaquet.

It was a long melancholy saga of decline and decay. Nevertheless, the Major said, there was no sense in whining at what was not to be helped. A soldier was always a soldier, plenty of decent fellows were still joining up, and there were good little wars running somewhere most of the time. And then young Francis, cool as a cucumber, had made his astounding and shattering declaration.

1

Towards the end of his last year at Harrow, he wrote that he had won a scholarship to Magdalen College, Oxford. That was the first intimation the Major had of his even trying for one, and he thought it a rummy uncalled-for thing to do. Still, men entered the Army from Oxford often enough, with no real harm to their future; and, after a polite congratulation, he said as much in his reply. Francis wrote again, confessing that he had no inclination for a military career at all, that he had long been aware of this fact, and hoping his father would understand.

The shock was all the greater because the boy's record at Harrow had been everything the Major could wish. Captain of cricket and rugger, head of his house and then of the School, he seemed as sound as a bell. True, the reports spoke highly of his work in class, but there was nothing in that. The Barracloughs had never been dunces, and the library at Castle More had rows of books, bound in leather, bestowed on them for proficiency in this, that, or the other, unread and disregarded. One there was, awarded for Divinity in 1856, in which the family did rejoice; but only because the winner was sacked on the following day for drunken shouts in chapel.

And Francis hoped his father would understand, did he? Had it been almost anything else, anything natural, like running up debts or getting the boot for tippling or wenching, this hope would have been fulfilled. But who can grasp a matter that lies completely beyond his range? The Major felt that he had never understood his son at all. He would have taken his oath, from professional experience rather than family pride, that Francis was cut out for a soldier. Not one of the qualities the Army looked for seemed to be lacking.

Could it be, he wondered now, that his own marriage had something to do with it? Towards the end of the War, with everyone mad and everything upside down, he had chosen a wife from an alien world altogether. Maria Fawcett was English, of excellent family and devoted to him; but, while there were statesmen, judges and bishops among her forbears, there had never been a single man in the Army. He had not held it against her at the time, indeed, they were blissfully happy. Several years, enough for anxiety, were to pass before Maria

2

conceived, but with the coming of Francis the only shadow was lifted. After her sudden death, when the boy was three, he never thought of her but with love and pain and longing. Nevertheless, with Francis behaving in this peculiar manner now, he could not help asking himself if the Fawcett blood were behind it, and if the Fawcett strain had been too much for his.

There was nothing whatever to be done, of course, except pray for a global war. He was not the man to cajole or grizzle, still less to threaten, even if any threat could be made. Apart from his scholarship and, no doubt the grants and hand-outs of this spoon-fed age, Francis had an income, left by his mother. At eighteen, he was his own master entirely; and to Magdalen he accordingly went.

As long as he was there, he spent part of every vacation at home in the west of Ireland. Purposeful as any old dowager, his father took care to throw the right sort of girl in his way. By now he had resigned his commission and retired to the family place; and his one hope was, to see Francis married to some dear creature from an appropriate stud, producing heirs to revive the Barraclough stock. Francis dined and danced and flirted with the baits that dangled before him, but it was all too clear that he had no serious intention. The Major did not despair, pinning his faith to the time when, his studies completed, the boy would come home for good.

But here too there was shock and disappointment. After graduating with a Double First, Francis abruptly declared he should move to Paris, to find himself, as he put it. What on earth could he mean by that? The Major was fond of reading and, in modern novels, had often been struck by the number of their heroes who went roaming about 'in search of an identity'. But they were of a type who hardly knew who their grandfathers were. No such gaps existed in the Barraclough information. And how in the world did Francis propose to find himself among the Frogs? The Major's loathing of France and her people was purely atavistic, but he put it down to wartime experience, and this new defection puzzled and hurt him almost as much as the other.

'Can't make it out, Maguire, can't make it out at all,' he

3

said one morning, gloomily. Maguire had been his batman in the Army and now was butler at the Castle: he was London Irish, an amalgam of A.1 soldier and servant with 3-star crackpot and detrimental, his faults redeemed, the Major felt, by his virtues, above all, by his unswerving loyalty.

'He'll see through that lot fast enough, sir,' Maguire replied.

'But what is he doing? What is he up to?'

'Shouldn't think he knows hisself.'

'I want him here. Hang it all, the family place, the only son. Most young men would be glad to be in his shoes.'

'That they would,' assented Maguire, with a glance through the window at the handsome prospect beyond. He'd have given his ears for a slice of it.

'No feeling for what has taken centuries to put together,' the Major went on. 'And when you think of what usually happens to houses like ours!' Sold up to the Government, the Church, to cattle dealers who only wanted the pasture and tore the fine old buildings down, to Hun hoteliers, or Japanese who fabricated biscuits out of seaweed and heaven knew what. 'Can he have picked up some Red ideas over there?'

'I wouldn't say so, sir. Clean, dressed proper, no beard, hair off the collar.'

'Yes, yes, they can be all that and still go to the devil, can't they? Look at poor Carrageen's son.'

'Look at Lord Carrageen, sir.'

'True.' The Major sighed and shook his head. 'I don't know. He surely couldn't . . . it would not be possible . . .'

'Not that, sir, no, not ever!' Maguire, deeply shocked, broke in.

The suggestion, too awful for either to put in words, was that young Francis feared for himself on political grounds. The break with England and the establishment of the republic had never been recognized by the family. They had always served the Crown, and saw no reason to change. And this may have been the very cause of their being left in comparative peace, through the various waves of trouble. Landlords who had stayed at home, managed their property and held the belief, so hideous to the Irish mind, that tenants should pay their rent, incurred such animosity that when at last the maddened natives

4

rose their descendants were shot or burned out. But the Barra-cloughs were mostly away at some war, leaving affairs to a bailiff who, once his own pockets were filled, respected the rights of the people. Thus their fortune had not been wrung from downtrodden serfs but amassed by the purses and other military plums of an age gone by, and by felicitous marriage: so that even the fertile popular mind had not been able to weave its legends about them.

Nevertheless, the troubles were on again, and worse than ever. And there was always that secret worry about the Fawcett strain. It was more than just the lack of soldiers in the family, too. In the bloody reign of Queen Mary a Fawcett bishop had reneged, rather than burn at the stake; and who was to know how many other shameful Fawcett doings there were, that had never come to light? The Major would often reproach himself for dreadful thoughts like these, but still, he could not absolutely put them away.

'Silly of me, of course not,' he said gruffly. 'But there must be something wrong. And I'm hanged if I can think what.'

'Permission to speak, sir?'

'Go ahead.'

'It's my belief, he's up in the air and needs a shock to bring him down.'

'A shock, Maguire? What sort of a shock?'

'A real bad 'un, sir, what would shake him to the toenails.'

'Hm.'

The Major let the subject drop and did not raise it again, but Maguire's thrust had gone home. Maguire had his little ways and weaknesses, but his view of any situation that did not involve himself was apt to be clear and sound. And this par-ticular judgement of his was timely. At present the Major was deep in a book which the Rector had lent him and which dealt with Zen Buddhism. It was not at all his line of country, but after the Rector assured him that most of the Japanese Staff in World War Two were adherents of the sect, he thought there might be something in it. Nor was he disappointed. That same morning he had come to the Zen method of clarifying the disciples' ideas and helping them towards illumination by whacking them over the head with a club. No tedious explana-

5

tion, no wearisome argument, simply, wham! It met with his entire approval, and now here was old Maguire, mysteriously in tune with the wisdom of the East! The Major said nothing, but thought the more, brooded and planned.

For his part, Maguire, having delivered himself in this manner, forgot all about it. Time slipped quietly past, weeks melting away one after the other, as they do in the country. Now and then, as he took in the morning's post, he saw a letter from Paris among it, and knew the Major's spirits would be heavy that day. Otherwise, life went on as usual, with hunting, shooting, business to do with the estate, parish affairs, the normal occupations of a Squire.

But then one morning, the Major was found by Maguire in the study, unconscious. He was slumped over the desk, on which lay the post, unopened. Maguire ran for a gardener and the pair of them carried him up to bed. The doctor was summoned immediately, but there was nothing he could do. After lying in a coma for a couple of weeks the Major gently expired, without coming round for an instant.

All through this time, Maguire was in a terrible way. It came back to him now, his saying that Mr Francis needed a shock, and the Irish half of his mind led him to think he was somehow to blame. And he had no idea where the young man was living, nor had anyone else. His address was not in the Major's book, nor could a single letter from him be found. Every drawer in every room that the Major used, Maguire turned out, but all to no avail. The Rector telephoned here and there, to Harrow, to Magdalen, to the British Consul in Paris. No one could tell him anything, and there seemed no earthly way of getting in touch with the boy. It was only after the death that Maguire remembered a crumpled note in the Major's hand when he found him. In the stress of the moment he had simply thrown it aside. Now he rushed up to the study and saw it there on the floor, the paper heavily creased, as if the Major had screwed it up, intending to throw it away himself. Maguire had trouble in making the contents out.

'Oh my Gawd!' he muttered, when he had deciphered it.

It was from Mr Francis, saying that he would marry in a fortnight's time – that meant, now! – one Marigold Portman,

6

native of South Carolina and a student at the Sorbonne. They had been engaged for the past six months, but for various reasons had not been able to fix a date for the wedding before. He was the happiest man alive. Please would his father come over at once and stay with him in his flat on the Quai Voltaire. The honeymoon was to be spent in the South of France.

Having taken this in, Maguire telephoned to the Rector in a daze, to pass on the news and give the young man's address. He begged him to take the steps required, feeling himself unequal to it. There was one shock after another that was what, and all his doing. That unlucky remark of his had called up an evil spirit and set these horrors in train. Why had he ever opened his mouth? Now he had lost the best and kindest master a man could have, and God only knew what would become of him, too old for the Army, or for anything but a Whitehall runabout or night-club Commissionaire.

There was in fact no means of telling how far, if at all, this communication bore on the stroke which had carried the Major off. A full-blooded man, fond of good cheer and given to hearty exercise, he had repeatedly been advised by the doctor to take things quietly. He had been urged to cut down his eating, drinking and smoking, to avoid any violent exertion and remember his age. But when people heard of its message, there was a tremendous amount of discussion. Those who knew of his matrimonial schemes for Francis – that is to say, the county at large – were in no doubt of the matter. American and a blue stocking, whom nobody knew, living in Paris, most likely à la Bohème, this Marigold Portman was not the woman to meet his specification. Even the Rector, whose charity was such that his opinions were all but worthless, looked grave; and Miss Hackle, whose lack of it made hers completely so, declared it was next door to murder.

Thus the telegram which Francis opened in his flat, expecting fatherly good wishes and details of the Major's arrival, informed him instead of his own bereavement and asked his immediate return for the funeral.

7

# Chapter Two

Francis had no idea of the turmoil he had caused his father, as the Major had kept it to himself. He had expected a battle over the Army, and been most agreeably surprised. The Major's reply, laconic and somehow impersonal as all his letters were, merely said it was up to him and left it at that. But the old boy had always been a brick and, with this question out of the way, Francis imagined the sky was clear. The amount of distress his subsequent doings occasioned would have horrified him, had he known of it. As often happens with parent and child, what to one was a mystery, to the other was all plain sailing.

If you were lucky – most people were not – to be in line for a decent property and money to keep it going, what more could you want? That was the riddle that teased and tore at the Major's mind, and for which neither he nor Maguire had been able to think of an answer. But it was not to drowse his youth away in the country, Francis held, that he had taken a Double First. He had his share of the Barraclough spirit and by no means despised his future prospects. They were some way off, however, and he was not going to settle tamely down as the son of the house meanwhile. He wanted all the things that the Major could never abide, a city, bustle, crowds, lights, conversation instead of gossip, brilliant men and beautiful girls who never got on a horse.

He thought that Paris would provide them and thither he went, explaining the move to his father in that unlucky phrase about finding himself: unlucky, in that it drew the single barbed rejoinder his parent had ever made. 'I was not aware that you were missing,' the Major wrote, 'be sure and let me know if you turn up.' When Francis read these words, he felt hot all over. From that day on, his letters home grew rare and brief, and entirely vague, except for the very last one he was ever to write.

That letter too was written in innocence, with no idea of its coming perhaps as a bombshell, the abrupt disclosure of a *fait accompli*. Francis was merely so wrapped up in himself and his happiness that he never dreamed of the effect it might have. When he and Marigold got engaged, she was about to take her finals at the Sorbonne and she had promised her folks at home not to marry until she had a degree. On this subject her father, no scholar himself, was slightly mad. The Portmans rolled in money and, further, clung to the old southern belief that ladies never went out to work. That degree was merely a frill, cachet, symbol, or 'some darned thing', as Marigold said, but she had given her promise. Were she to fail . . . The couple were on tenterhooks until they heard that she had passed; then they fixed the wedding with a minimum of delay. To the amusement of their friends, they had continued living chastely apart up to now, losing more than enough precious time, and they proposed to make up for it at once.

Everything was done in a tearing hurry, authorities notified, the time of the ceremony fixed, the Lutèce booked for the reception, rooms taken for a honeymoon in Provence, clothes ordered and fitted at curious hours, driving tailors and dressmakers to madness, invitations cabled to friends abroad, inclining them to suspect a shot-gun affair, Marigold's flat relinquished, the landlord threatening to sue: they had never worked so hard in their lives. And now, after all that, with matters settled at last, there came the Rector's wire as Francis lay blissfully dreaming on the sofa in his flat.

His first reaction to the news did him no credit at all. He felt that it was just too bad of his father to have done such a thing at such a time. His second was even worse. He was tempted to say nothing about it, tell Marigold that his father was ill and could not come, breaking the news only when they were married and on their way to the south. But he soon realized that this was out of the question, as well as disgraceful. All attempts to fool his bride were doomed to failure, as he had discovered already. He telephoned to her flat, but of course she was out, busy with last-minute preparations. They were to meet for lunch at a *bistrot* on the Quai and he would somehow have to contain himself until then.

When she arrived, he was already, drinking black coffee

with cognac, smoking fast and looking pale and distracted. Without a word he thrust the telegram at her, stubbed out a half-finished cigarette and promptly lit up again while she read it through. Having done so, she folded it up, put it away and quietly reached for the menu.

'Have you ordered?' she asked in her gentle drawl.

'*Ordered?* Of course not.'

She said no more for a moment or two, thinking things over. Then, 'I just can't figure out,' she remarked, 'why you are so upset.'

'Darling girl, what else should I be?' he exploded. 'My father, suddenly dead . . .'

She communed with herself further awhile, as if passing a complex situation under review. Francis had never spoken about his father or anything to do with home. From time to time, however, she had noticed letters with Irish stamps on them lying about in his flat for days, unopened. It did not altogether fit in with a display of filial grief.

'Yes, but,' she resumed, 'that's not what has really upset you.'

Francis opened his mouth to give an indignant denial, then shut it again. Now the waiter bustled up, and Marigold asked for a mushroom omelette, chicory salad, a strawberry tart and a quarter of wine.

'How can you eat?' he groaned.

'It isn't the end of the world,' she replied. 'Just think, three weeks ago we weren't sure we could marry at all until goodness knows when. Daddy would never have given way.'

'Parents! If it isn't one thing, it's another.'

'Well, your father didn't plan this, poor fellow. And the funeral is not until the day after tomorrow. We can still be married in the morning, and you can take an afternoon plane. We need only put the honeymoon off a while.'

'Are you serious?' Francis cried. 'I wrote to my father a fortnight ago. He will have spread the news at once. Everyone will expect the wedding to be postponed for ages.'

'Does it matter who expects what? Seems like our own personal business.'

10

'There is no such thing as "own personal business" in Ireland,' he told her grimly.

'But Francis, think of the fuss if we cancel everything now. My parents are flying in from the States this minute. And I can't see that anyone your side has to hear about the wedding at all. You just attend the funeral and come on back.'

It was a strange idea that she had of Irish procedures! Francis wished with all his heart that he knew as little. 'My dearest girl, it won't be as easy as you imagine. Family affairs, no end of to-do . . . Once I'm there, I'll stick like a cow in a bog. God only knows when I'd see you again!'

'Well then, I'll come along too,' said Marigold cheerfully. 'And if there are any troublemakers, we'll tell them to go jump in the lake.'

'Quite impossible! Not to be thought of.' A nightmare vision of them both, newly wed at the funeral with the eyes of the County fixed upon them, flitted across his brain. He signalled to the waiter and ordered another cognac.

'And bring him a *bifteck saignant*, with *frites* as well,' said Marigold. 'And some wine. Now now, Francis, you know you're starving. What's impossible about me coming too? I'm not settling down here, a wife in name only, while you stick in that bog you mentioned. No, sir!'

'Darling, I'm terribly sorry, it just wouldn't do. We'll have the wedding all right, as you suggested, but then I shall go on alone. Forgive me for throwing my weight about! But matters like this you must leave to me.' He spoke with firm male decision, but smiled at her and stroked her hand to take away any sting his marital authority might have caused.

At ten o'clock on the following night, the Dublin plane with them both aboard was preparing to land. Rain beat furiously against the windows and the lights of the city were blotted out. A woman's voice reeled off a series of gutteral sounds and then, softly in English, thanked all present for flying with the line and asked them to do so again. The passengers were mainly homebound tourists, with a sprinkling of priests and nuns who crossed themselves devoutly at the reassuring bump of the aircraft on the runway. Various of the men were flushed and

11

appeared to be steaming, like newly boiled lobsters, their eyes set in their heads. Pretty hostesses undid their belts and smilingly helped them to the gangway.

'Are those poor fellows ill?' asked Marigold.

'No,' said Francis. 'Just in a funk.' Their condition gave rise to a train of sombre thought. 'Darling, can you bear this taxi drive? It's ten to one against anyone being sober at this hour. We could go to the hotel here, if you'd rather, and start at crack of dawn.'

'But don't they expect us at the other end?'

'Up to a point, yes. But no one really expects anything here, until it happens. It's a filthy night, too.' The rain lashed them both as they tore to the airfield bus. 'And you must be worn to a frazzle.'

'It's been quite a day,' she agreed. 'But I'm for going on now we've got as far as this. It'll be something to tell our grandchildren.'

'That's rather looking ahead, isn't it?' He was living very much in the present himself. 'But you're a game little job, I must say.'

Despite her fatigue, Marigold was enjoying the experience immensely. The rain, the priests and nuns, the drunks, the brogue, all fitted in with what she had heard of the country and, as usual with newcomers, all met with her approval. The bus now deposited them at the main building, which she found as cute as a doll's house; and when they were herded with all the rest to the agricultural officials, she was enraptured by the purpose behind it.

'But even if I did go walking over a farm where there's Foot and Mouth,' she crowed, when the soles of her elegant footwear were thoroughly sprayed, 'I'd hardly do it in these! Don't they ever stop to think, people might have more than one pair?'

'It's just a ritual,' Francis said. 'I imagine they don't think at all.'

'And did you hear that man, telling us lift up our feet "one at a time"? I'm going to have to keep a diary!'

Accustomed to nonsense from birth, Francis found nothing comical in it. His thoughts in any case were gloomily fixed on the nightmare journey ahead. Two hundred odd miles, with a

12

tipsy joker at the wheel ... But when, after passing the Customs, they reached the exit the first thing he saw, stiff as a ramrod, stony-faced as a Guard at the Palace, was the figure of Maguire. If an angel had sprung up in his path, he could not have been more astounded and overjoyed; in all his imaginings of what was to come, the idea of being met had not occurred once.

Maguire stepped forward and touched his cap. 'Good evening, sir.'

'Good evening, Maguire. Nice to see you. Have you come to fetch us?'

'Sir.'

'Good man yourself.' It sounded, in his ears, like his father talking. 'This is my wife, Maguire.'

'Good evening, ma'am. If you'll allow me.' He took Marigold's hand luggage and signalled to a porter. 'The car is just by the entrance, sir.'

'Things are never as bad as one expects them to be,' said Marigold happily, snuggling up to Francis as the car started off. She held this view because any time that they were, she immediately forgot: it was a matter of temperament rather than observation. 'You're looking very solemn. Are you returning thanks? Should I be silent?'

He smiled and was about to give her a kiss when he caught Maguire's expresionless eye in the mirror and refrained. His mind was in a whirl. There had been so much to occupy it since the fatal wire arrived that certain matters had altogether been overlooked. With his father dead, he still was thinking of himself as a son, and a thoroughly bad one. Well might Marigold wonder what had 'really' upset him! it was the simple fact of being so little upset, of not being able to feel much more than he did. And when he spoke to her of family affairs to settle, he had only meant such tangles and worries as follow every death. But all that was suddenly changed by the appearance and demeanour of Maguire. Never before had the Major's batman addressed him otherwise than as 'Mr Francis'. The 'sir' had abruptly brought it home that he was the heir and new master, he was Barraclough of Castle Reef, driving along in his own car with his own man at the wheel: Maguire's coming

13

to fetch him had not been an act of kindly consideration, but part of a servant's duty.

'I was wondering how you will like the house,' he said.

'Why, yes. It's not as if you ever stopped talking about it. Garrulous as a clam !'

'I just didn't think of going there, somehow. Of course, we should have done, sooner or later.' He sighed.

'Is it that bad? Tell me the worst. Is it a ruin?' The prospect seemed not to appal her.

'Not quite. But there are very few modern conveniences.'

'A cabin?' she asked in delight. 'A sweet little whitewashed cabin, on the edge of a lake? With a thatched roof?'

'I'm afraid not. There's a lake all right. Perhaps you'd better wait and see.'

With that she had to be content. Very soon the pair of them were asleep, Marigold so soundly that she never woke up at the journey's end. Francis carried her across the threshold into the hall, reflecting wryly that this was the only wedding-night custom he would have much chance to observe.

'You are in Spion Kop, sir,' said Maguire, who showed no trace of fatigue. 'I'll bring up the luggage. There's cold supper ready, if you wish.'

'No thanks, we ate on the plane. Is the . . . is my . . .'

'The Major's coffin is in the church, sir. The Rector will call in the morning.'

It was the hell of a night for a newly married pair. Francis undressed his sleeping wife and put her to bed, got in beside her and lay thinking dreary thoughts until sleep overcame him too.

# Chapter Three

The rain streamed down the whole night through, as if the very heavens were nothing but water. Then as morning broke it stopped, suddenly and completely, in the capricious way of these parts. The clouds, their business done, quickly made off and a perfect double rainbow spanned the sky; and an hour or so later, as Dr Thornton left the Rectory, the whole country was beaming under a soft September sun.

A Divine mercy, the Rector thought; a Divine mercy indeed. Nothing would have kept the parishioners from the Major's funeral, were they to be drenched to the skin, and carried off by pneumonia themselves. Most were elderly, some were ailing, but to a man and a woman they would have been there. What a downpour! What a downpour! As he walked up the garden path, his practised eye took in the ravages made on his flower-beds. He had staked the chrysanthemums and dahlias on the previous afternoon–another mercy!–but the gladioli and asters were beaten to earth, and the pansies were in a miniature pond.

In the orchard a shower of raindrops fell upon him from a tree. He looked up vaguely and saw that the branches were practically stripped of fruit. But that could not have been due to the storm. The plums, President, were far from ripe and would not have been shaken off their boughs so easily; and there were torn twigs and trampled leaves scattered about on the earth below. No, it was the boys again, those naughty boys. If they wanted fruit they had only to ask him, as they very well knew; but if they must help themselves, why not taste a couple before they stripped the tree? They will not think, he mused, young people so rarely will. Now the whole crop was wasted, and he was fond of the President himself. The next tree to it was a Gage, loaded with fruit all ripe and sweet as honey, but the green colour must have put them off and they had gone for the deceptive purple of the others. Strange, with all their experience, how they never learned which trees to rob!

Busy with his thoughts, we had reached the end of the garden and turned into the road which led to the Castle. From her cottage window Miss Hackle saw him coming and hurried out,

15

as her practice was, to engage him in conversation: it was one
of the little crosses he had to bear. Her theme this morning,
however, was neither the state of her health nor the doings of
her Siamese cat.

'He is here,' she began. 'Arrived at three this morning!'

'Poor young man, he must be tired,' the Rector said mildly.

'He has brought a young woman with him,' Miss Hackle
continued, lowering her voice.

She was supernaturally well-informed, the Rector could not
but consider: it was barely nine o'clock, when most people
were still at their breakfast. 'I think we knew he was engaged
to be married,' he said, in the same tone as before.

'But after all that has happened! To bring her here! I
wonder she had the heart to come.'

'Francis does not know all that has happened,' the Rector
said. 'We had no means of getting in touch with him, until
Maguire remembered that letter. And, Miss Hackle, if it comes
to that, what do we know ourselves, except that his father had
a stroke?'

'The poor dear old Major!' Hiss Hackle moaned. 'Though
why do I call him old? Struck down in the prime of life!'

'We none of us know when the hour may come,' the Rector
replied. 'And Dr McLeod had been anxious about him for
some time past. That is a fact, while anything else can only be
supposition. Miss Hackle, a dear friend and neighbour of us all
is gone. Today we shall pay him our last respects. Let us leave
all other matters to those whom they concern.'

He smiled at her to soften the little rebuke and, raising his
hat, walked on. Miss Hackle was a model parishioner as far as
cleaning or decorating the church, playing the harmonium at
the services and turning up for vestry meetings, went; but her
way of always thinking the worst was hardly Christian. She
thought it because she wanted to, and nothing could ever
persuade her that she was wrong. Still, who was he to talk?
and what kind of a Christian? All that the Gospel taught of
death and the life hereafter, he truly believed; nevertheless,
he was sad this morning, sad as a pagan, as if the lovely sunlit
world around him were the only one and death, a final extinc-
tion. Very soon now he would say those tremendous words, 'I
am the resurrection and the life' – with a heart as heavy as

16

lead. No, no, it ill became him to find faults in others.

From the Rectory to Castle Reef was a short mile, the way leading over an old arched bridge, a torrent foaming and tumbling beneath, and along the river bank to the wrought iron gates of the demesne. As he walked up the avenue under the weeping elms, his thought went back to the day when Arthur first came back with his bride. He saw them as clearly as if they were standing before him now, the handsome gay young soldier and the bewitching girl, with her great dark dreamy eyes and the air, which she never lost, of not quite belonging. Her charm bowled everyone over, but there had always been something, she had always struck the neighbourhood as an unlikely match for Arthur. Then Francis was born, and he had christened him amid great rejoicing, Arthur bursting with love and pride: then came the cruel sudden death of Maria not long afterwards; and then Francis began to grow up, looking more like his father year by year, a true Barraclough and worthy successor until . . .

But the world was changing, as it must, the Rector thought, climbing the steps to the front door and, Irish fashion, going straight in. He was an old man, well past seventy. Things could not go on as they always had, could not repeat themselves over and over ad infinitum. There was no one to blame, no one had done any wrong. But, in the hall of the big silent house that he had known so full of life, the memory of that happy young pair came back again.

As he stood there, his eyes shut, with the past running through his head like a film, a gentle voice addressed him.

'Good morning,' it said. 'I think you must be the Rector.'

Abruptly recalled to the present, somewhat confused, he opened his eyes and turned to the speaker. What he saw, half made him think he must be daydreaming still. It was not that the girl was lovely, with her long blue dark-lashed eyes and magnolia skin, but that, with no real facial resemblance, she reminded him poignantly of Maria, in the way she carried herself, in her touch of foreignness, in the sense of her having blown in from somewhere far away. Francis was too young when Maria died to remember the least thing about her. There was no question of him trying to find, as men so often did, his mother in his wife. He had simply picked her out, as Arthur

17

had picked out Maria, because she was what he wanted: apparently, things did repeat themselves after all!

'Are you surprised to see me?' Marigold was asking. 'Francis brought me along. He's only just woken up, yesterday was kind of tough, but he'll be down in a minute. I'm exploring! He never told me he lived in a palace. Come on in, to the drawing-room, I've located that much.'

At a loss for words, the Rector followed her meekly and they both sat down.

'You *are* surprised, I can see,' Marigold went on. 'Francis thought you would be. I suppose all this is rather unconventional.'

'Not at all, no, no,' the Rector assured her. 'Young people do travel about together these days, it is quite the usual thing. It was very different in my time, but I can see no harm in it. You must, of course, be his fiancée.' And he gave her a fatherly smile, intended to put her at her ease.

Marigold was at her ease already, indeed, she was seldom anywhere else. 'Why, no,' she said. 'I'm his wife.'

The Rector was so startled that he dropped his hat on the floor.

'His wife,' he echoed, in dismay. 'In the eyes of God, perhaps?' he suggested hopefully.

'I guess so,' Marigold drawled. 'But anyhow, in the eyes of the French Civil Service.'

'But my dear young lady, we understood that your wedding was fixed for yesterday,' the Rector cried, in mounting agitation. 'That is what Francis wrote to his father. Do you mean to tell me that ... that ...'

'We went ahead? Why, yes. We figured it was the only thing to do. Francis said he'd have business here, and didn't know when he'd be back. And all our arrangements were made.'

'Oh dear!' said the Rector faintly. 'Oh dear, dear, dear!'

Miss Hackle seemed to rise up through the floor, like the demon king in a pantomime, and confront him with folded arms.

'I certainly am sorry if it was wrong,' Marigold said. 'Francis was worried about it, but I talked him over. My parents were on their way from the States when the telegram came, and there were friends flying in from Oxford and London. I'd

18

given notice at my apartment and moved my things round to Francis. We'd fixed the wedding at the *mairie* and the reception at a hotel. So, as we were going to be married anyway some time, it seemed like ordinary sense.' She said nothing of how, to the grief of her parents and the general disappointment, they had rushed away from the reception after a bare half-hour, nor of the cancelled honeymoon.

Arrangements, arrangements and ordinary sense: what were such things as these, weighed against a proper respect for the dead and compliance with custom? The Rector, unhappily aware of the gulf between himself and this charming girl, tried not to let his feelings show.

'What is done, is done,' he said kindly. 'It was a difficult position, indeed. You were married at the "Mary", you say. Is that an English or an American church? I do not remember hearing of it.'

'The *mairie*? It's French for town hall,' said Marigold.

'Town hall? A registry office?' quavered the Rector, with a sense of the very ground giving way beneath him. 'You were married by the civil authorities?'

'You have to be, in France,' she explained. 'If you want a religious ceremony too, you can have it, but separately.'

Apparently, they had *not* desired one. That was a terrible thing, to be sure. But at least the scandal would not be so great, as they were not really married at all. How the poor Rector did wish he had kept the news from Paris to himself! Maguire had passed it on to him as the man in charge, and there was no need to spread it further. He had innocently done so, however, and in next to no time the parish was all a-buzz . . .

At this moment Francis came in, and reminded him of the purpose for which he had come. He rose at once and hurried towards him, his eyes moistening and his hands outstretched.

'My dear boy!' he said, with a break in his voice. 'I fear this has been a terrible shock, and a sad coming home. You have been so much in all our thoughts.'

'I never knew my father was even unwell,' Francis said. 'He never mentioned himself when he wrote. I thought your telegram was from him, to say he was coming over. Couldn't think why it took him so long to reply.'

The Rector gave him a carefully pruned account of what

19

had taken place. 'And you see, none of us knew where to find you,' he said. 'I rang the Consul in Paris, but you had not been registered there. But for Maguire's luckily thinking of that letter, we could not have reached you at all.' Now he saw that Francis was turning deathly white. 'My poor boy, all this is a fearful strain. I am sorry indeed to break in upon you, but, as you know, certain things have to be settled.'

'When is the funeral?'

'I have fixed it, provisionally, for three o'clock. But everyone is standing by, in case you prefer a somewhat later hour.'

'Three o'clock will do very well.' He wished he knew what on earth to say next. 'This is my wife, as she has probably told you.'

'Indeed, she has, we were chatting away before you came in. I am sure she will be the greatest comfort and support.'

'Maguire and Mrs Jeffars between them have made a few preparations. My father's friends will be welcome here, afterwards, if you will kindly tell them so.'

'Certainly, certainly.' The Rector's heart was failing him again. 'But they won't expect it, in view of the short notice. And they may well think it kinder to leave you to yourselves.'

Francis understood him perfectly. 'Just as they please.'

The Rector then declared that he must be going and was halfway to the door when Francis called after him. 'Oh, Dr Thornton, by the way! I'm afraid I haven't any suitable clothes. I shall have to come as I am.'

'As you are!' exclaimed the Rector, with a horrified glance at him. He was wearing the festive light-blue suit intended for Aix-en-Provence. 'My dear Francis, I am sorry to raise the matter at such time, but this simply will not do.'

'I can hardly get it dyed by the afternoon,' said Francis, gritting his teeth.

'But surely you can find something else? You will shock the whole parish!'

'If the parish has nothing worse to shock it . . .' Francis was bursting out, when Marigold intervened.

'We'll fix something, Rector, don't worry. Francis never thought he was going to bury his father, you know, not for years and years.'

'Quite right, Mrs Barraclough, of course he did not and I

beg his pardon,' the Rector humbly replied. 'But one does have to be so careful. Things of no importance in themselves do have such far-reaching effects. I will leave it in your capable hands.' Despondently, he made his way out.

'And what are you proposing to fix?' growled Francis, when he had gone.

'Your father must have some dark clothes somewhere. Are you about the same height?'

'Yes, exactly the same – but he was three stone heavier.'

'OK, OK, a tuck here and a dart there. A few inverted pleats, maybe, and some buttons shifted. You didn't know I was a tailor, as well as everything else?'

'You're an angel and I'm a beast,' said Francis ruefully. 'But oh my God, did you ever hear the like of it? My suit, the parish, the scandal. No one thinks of anything here but of what people are going to say. And all the while, the poor old ass is practically brokenhearted.'

'I think he's a dear, and very original,' Marigold replied. 'He was charmed with me as long as he thought we were living in sin. But when I told him we were married, he got all upset. That's not how the pastors see it at home.'

'The parish again.'

'You say "parish" like you meant the Mafia or the KKK. I'm not losing my sleep for any parish. Now, you go and rummage in the wardrobes. How do I get a needle and thread?'

'Ah yes.' Francis walked across to the fireplace and touched a bell.

'What are you doing now?'

'What do you suppose?' The door opened and Maguire appeared. 'Sewing things for my wife, please, Maguire.'

'Sir.' Maguire withdrew.

'Well!' Marigold was actually looking impressed.

'Did you never see anyone ring a bell before?' asked Francis, amused.

'I may have done,' she replied. 'But I certainly don't recall a bell being answered. I'm going to enjoy this place. Well, off with you, there's no time to lose. You have to be made acceptable to this parish of yours before the clock strikes three.'

21

# Chapter Four

The church of St Andrew in Ballinaween, built in the days of
Protestant strength, was much too big for the number using it
now. This afternoon, however, it was full to overflowing.
Mourners had come from far and wide, from England and
Scotland too; as well as the few relations, there were men from
the Major's old regiment, hunting and shooting friends, boon
companions of one sort and another. All rose to their feet as
Francis came in, and it seemed to him as he walked up the aisle
that he knew hardly anyone there. He had never expected a
throng of that sort: he had never realized how well his father
was liked; and it deepened a weird sense that he had, of not
having really known him at all.

He took chief mourner's place in the front pew, left vacant
for him, behind the coffin. This was draped in the regimental
colours, with the Major's sword and medals on top. That was
Maguire, of course, trust Maguire. Miss Hackle was at her
harmonium to one side, all in black, and he bowed to her,
receiving the merest inclination of her censorious head. The
Kinsmen in the pew behind, to whom he turned next, responded in friendly fashion, shaking hands and murmuring
words of regret; but it occurred to him, they should all have
been staying at the Castle, and not one of them was. The rooms
prepared by Mrs Jeffars as a matter of course were all un-
occupied, as if the old customs had gone out with his father.

Now the Rector was coming in, all togged up, proclaiming
in his reedy old voice that he was the resurrection and the life
. . . ah, look here, this was not the moment for satire. The man
believed what he said, and no doubt the worthy congregation
believed it too. All the same, Francis thought, the old boy kept
a foot on the ground: for as he passed him by he shot a glance
in his direction, relaxing visibly at what he saw. Marigold had
worked with a will, and Francis was decorously clad in
elephant grey. And more than the colour was elephantine, he

reflected. A spaciousness in the seat had defied her best endeavours, and, viewed from the rear, he must be looking a clown.

Again he reproached himself for having thoughts so inappropriate, tried to fix them on the service, tried to feel something of what he ought to be feeling, of what everyone there would assume he felt. But it was all to no purpose. The whole way though the splendid liturgy – the Rector would have none of that modern mess – and even afterwards at the committal, his mind went skipping about in the same deplorable manner; and, at one particularly solemn point, he had a sudden crazy desire to laugh. That did shame him, deeply, for a while; but soon he was off again, remembering how the bullfighter Belmonte also had written in his Memoirs of being seized with inward mirth at the side of a yawning grave. Belmonte: then on to other books, on to Marigold, their wedding, Paris at night, the flowers of Aix-en-Provence ... wretch as he was, he simply could not help it.

The Rector, his duties accomplished, had a few words of comfort for him.

'You must think of your father as with you still,' he said, 'watching over you, knowing your inmost thoughts, loving you always. You were everything to him while he was here. You know it, and the knowledge will help you bear the separation.'

I shall go mad, but mad, but mad, thought Francis. Does he want me to? Will no one rid me ... He pulled himself together and warmly thanked the kind old man. 'Will you come back to the house, Rector? Do! I wouldn't let Marigold come, but I know she would like to see you.'

'Of course, dear boy, with pleasure. If you can wait a moment while I disrobe, I shall be glad of a lift in your car.'

Weary and sad as he was, he meant to give the poor young fellow what support he could. The invitation to the parish had been duly passed on, and glumly received, and he feared a general boycott. He did not blame the parishioners; he never blamed anyone, and the local feeling was but natural. Nevertheless, he could not bear to think of Francis and that delightful girl waiting in their empty house for the guests who never came.

As often happened, however, in his simple way he had misjudged the affair entirely. The parish was scandalized, aggrieved, indignant, but at the same time it was bursting with curiosity. The scandal itself was a welcome break in the all too even tenor of country life, and heads would be happily shaking over it for months to come; but in order to do it justice, it was essential to know a great deal more. You could hardly take the bride to pieces before you had met her. And then Francis himself was an enigma, what was he up to, what were his plans, what sort of fellow would he turn out to be? Would he, for instance – worried his godfather the MFH – be as good a friend to the Hunt as his father had been? Would he, other men asked themselves, preserve the coverts as keenly, maintain and stock the river, inviting his neighbours to shoot and fish at will? Would he, the ladies were anxious to know, allow their jumble sales to be held in the Park, and, as the Major had promised to do, put central heating in the church? All in all, whatever the rights and wrongs of the case, it was not a moment for the hugging of grievances.

Apart from the parish, there were the kinsmen and friends from abroad, who had not the least idea of the local convulsions and would not have cared a straw if they had. Thus, when the Barraclough car set off, it was followed by every soul who had been present in church, including, after some inner conflict, Miss Hackle.

'I hope the refreshments will go round!' remarked Francis, wishing he could find something to say that was not completely banal.

'Loaves and fishes!' beamed the Rector. The unexpected triumph of charity over resentment had filled his heart with innocent joy.

I daresay! Thought Francis. 'How's the cellar, Maguire?' he asked.

'Not too bad, sir. We'll manage.'

Mrs Jeffars had sized things up already and streaked off before the committal, availing herself of Poacher's Gap in the high stone wall round the Park for a quick sprint home to her kitchen. There, in a frenzy, she opened tins, cut sandwiches, put kettles to boil, polished decanters and goblets of the fine old

Waterford glass, while Juno the Irish wolfhound looked on, puzzled and disapproving.

'Wouldn't you know, they'd never miss anything going?' Mrs Jeffars panted. She habitually passed remarks to the dog that she would not have breathed to another. 'Didn't I say as much to Maguire, and mightn't I just as well be talking to the wall? O Sacred Heart of Jesus! here they come!'

Juno gave a growl of commiseration.

Maguire strode in and halted, staring about him like one in a dream. 'Cellar keys! Cellar keys!' he snapped. 'Where are them ruddy cellar keys?'

'Hanging there, before your nose, in their rightful place.' The airs of the chancer, she reflected, not like the poor dear Major, God rest and reward him!

'First time they ever were that!' He marched off, rattling the keys, and returned with a basketful of bottles.

While the pair of them seethed and fretted and the motorcade advanced, Marigold was upstairs, asleep in bed. Francis had told her that one or two friends, at most, might come on after the funeral and she wanted to rest a little before she received them. But the fevered rush of the day before and the long night journey had been very tiring, and the several hours work she put in on the Major's suit had finished her off. No sooner was her head on the pillow than she fell asleep, confusedly dreaming, until the commotion outside began.

Suddenly roused in her strange surroundings, she could not immediately think where she was. She lay on a large four-poster bed, like something out of Versailles, in a great high-ceilinged room with massive cupboards and chests and a chandelier. Under the spell of her last vivid dream, that of running round Dublin airport in a bridal gown, pursued by officials who wanted to spray her, she wondered vaguely how she had ever got here. Then she saw the luggage, her own and her husband's, and everything came slowly to mind. But what was all the kerfuffle below, engines, car doors slamming, voices, footsteps on the gravel, mounting the steps, tramping into the hall? She got up and wearily moved to the window. So that was what Francis meant by one or two at the most – a throng of people, and a procession of automobiles, stretching as far as the eye

25

could see! And they accused the Irish of exaggeration! Well, it was just too bad, but she was going to get right back on that museum-piece of a bed and stay there.

Before she was able to do so, however, Francis came bounding into the room. 'What's all this?' he cried. 'Hurry up and get dressed! Everybody is here.'

'You said there'd be one or two,' she observed. 'Seems more like a Convention of Moose to me.'

'That was the Rector's fault, he always gets everything wrong. Come on, do make haste. They are all dying to see you.'

'Couldn't I hold a kind of levée up here?' But she was slipping her nightdress off and looking round for her clothes as she spoke. 'Funny thing, I pictured married life as somehow different.'

'Well, you took me for better or worse,' he teased her, trying to help her pull some garment on.

'Hey, you're slowing me up! And there's nothing about better or worse in the Code Napoléon. They only made me promise to follow you around. As long as I do that, there's nothing to stop me bawling you out on the way.'

'Stop nattering. What shall you wear?'

'The gold brocade? No, that's too jazzy. The opal silk.'

'That's fine. Oh, how I do wish we could just stay here together!'

'Why yes. We could do that all right, couldn't we, except that we have to do something else.'

'You need a glass of wine.'

'Pardon me, it's not a glass I need, it's a barrel.'

The drawing-room had been made ready for such visitors as might appear, but it filled at once, and so did the summer parlour across the hall, and the hall itself. This was broad and lofty, the principal rooms on the floor above arranged as a gallery, with a noble flight of stairs at the further end. Unless they sneaked down by a back way, the pair had no choice but to descend this flight in ceremonial fashion, before the large attentive audience in the hall.

As they paused for a moment on the top stair, all heads turned upwards and all conversation died away. Francis took Marigold's arm in his, and gave it a gentle squeeze.

26

'*Courage, mon vieux, le diable est mort,*' he murmured.

'Can I rely on that?' She sounded none too sure.

Gingerly they went on down, as two young gladiators might approach an arena swarming with hungry lions. Very soon, however, Francis noted something odd in the reaction of those he had thought would be most hostile, his father's friends and coevals. All were gazing at Marigold, of course, but not critically or offensively, rather, as if she were a huge and pleasant surprise. What on earth had they expected? A cocotte from the Place Pigalle? A quadroon? An incipient schoolmarm, with spectacles and prominent teeth? She was looking a picture, as usual, but was that any cause for amazement? Was he so ugly himself, so deprived of all charm, that only a hag would accept him?

Nearest the foot of the stairs was Colonel Beaulieu, MFH, who appeared to be in a kind of daze.

'Thank you for coming, godfather,' Francis said. 'This is my wife.'

'Course I came, what next? Very sad business – I mean, congratulations, wish you joy, that sort of thing. How are you, my dear?' He looked distractedly round for his wife in the crowd, and called to her. 'Ruth! Ruth! Come over here and meet Maria.'

'Marigold,' said Mrs Barraclough, sweetly.

'Marigold, of course, charming name! Come and meet Marigold, Ruth.'

Mrs Beaulieu came over and promptly lost her bearings as well. 'Welcome to Ballinaween, Maria,' she said. 'I hope you will be very happy.'

'Her name is Marigold,' Francis smiled. A lot of old shandy-pates, that's what they were. But it was already clear that nothing would be as bad as expected, no gauntlets had to be run. As he moved among the guests so easily, the image of his father all those years ago, proudly displaying his wife, he felt a surge of goodwill towards them on every side. Even Miss Hackle, who had come prepared with a dig about the funeral bakéd meats, forwent her pleasure and offered the couple a Siamese kitten. People's minds turned back to happy far-off days, as if they had somehow come again; and it was felt that Francis,

27

whatever he had done or left undone, was a Barraclough through and through.

As for Marigold, quite apart from the effect of her appearance, she was a sensation. Americans, in the local view, were a noisy bumptious rabble, of Irish peasant stock, coarsened further by expatriation, who prowled up and down for traces of Biddy this or Paddy that, searching for what they called their roots. An American who was also a lady had never been known here before and, as with the Rector and the Beaulieus, her exotic air, her difference, brought memories of Maria to them all. The men went over like ninepins, and the women felt crude and homespun, until her warmth and charming manner revived their confidence. To all, that is, except Lord Carageen, a tireless old rip, who was merely put in mind of some little peach he had run after somewhere.

What had promised to be a major ordeal proved a happy occasion, overcast by the Major's loss, but auguring well for the future.

'Nothing is ever as bad as you think it will be,' Marigold said, sleepily, reverting to this favourite theme when the guests had all departed. She was lying on a Chesterfield in the drawing-room, her eyes opening and shutting like those of a drowsy cat. 'I thought I should doze off on my feet, like a cab-horse, but somehow I kept going.'

'You were utterly marvellous,' said Francis with fervour. 'What can I do for you?'

'You can give me that glass of wine. I didn't start drinking before. Mrs Jeffars did wonders, didn't she? There was enough for them all. But shouldn't we go help her clear the things away?'

'Lord, no. She'd be frightfully upset.'

'All very feudal,' Marigold drawled, sipping her wine. 'Maguire, now, he's like some Hollywood butler, except they'd get it all wrong. Where did you find him?'

'He was my father's batman all the while he was in the Army, and came back with him here. Doglike devotion, and so on. My father saved his life once, or so my cousin said. He never spoke of it himself. But he thought the world of him, anyhow.'

'No one could really be as deadpan as that. I wonder what he's like underneath?'

But Francis never stopped to imagine what servants were like underneath. 'Darling, what now? Another glass? Some dinner?'

'No, I guess it's me for Spion Kop and oblivion. I'm sorry, Mr Barraclough, looks like you'll have to keep your virginity one night more.' With a huge yawn, she dropped her glass and went suddenly off to sleep like a baby.

Francis carried her upstairs, undressed her and put her to bed. Really, he thought, it was getting to be a routine. But he was tired enough himself and very soon was peacefully unconscious beside her. Below stairs, Mrs Jeffars toiled away, washing up and tidying. Maguire was in his own small lair nearby watching television, with a bottle of the Major's Scotch at his elbow and a glass in his hand, smoking one of the Major's cigars. It was his usual custom of an evening, but Mrs Jeffars was greatly shocked by his observance of it now.

'Wouldn't you think he'd show a little respect?' she enquired of Juno, who lazily opened one eye and shut it again. 'And the poor dear Major, hardly cold in his grave!'

'When you're done chatting to yourself,' Maguire called out, 'you can bring in another siphon.'

'The Lord save us!' Mrs Jeffars gasped. 'If he hasn't the nerve of Old Nick!'

She brought the soda and banged it down on the table, Maguire clicking his tongue at the noise. Then she went back to work until the glass and china was all put away and the kitchen spotless. After that, she knelt on a wooden chair and, resting her arms on the back, said the rosary twice, the repeat for the Major, before she retired to bed. Maguire polished the whisky off at his leisure and went up as well.

For a time there was perfect peace. It was a calm night with never a branch stirring and not a cloud in the sky. Slowly the moon came up, the full golden harvest moon, to shed its radiance over the slumbering world. Then there arose, one by one, odd little sounds, as of an orchestra tuning or a singer trying his notes. Presently, all of a sudden, they joined in a full chorus, a thrilling rise and fall of voices, rich and sweet and

29

impassioned, an outpouring of weird inarticulate fervour. It woke the young couple in Spion Kop and Marigold, startled, sat bolt upright in bed.

'What on earth is that?' she cried.

'Only foxhounds, baying the moon,' Francis said. 'The Hunt begged one of our stables for them. Did you never hear it before?'

'Hear *that* before? I surely did not. Sounds like the banshee. And you tell me, it's only dogs!'

'Hounds, hounds!' he gently reproved her.

'Will they go on all night?'

'No, half an hour at the most.'

'Kind of *folklorique*! This is quite some place. Whoever could sleep in the midst of that hullabaloo?'

'Who indeed?' said Francis, rolling over and taking her in his arms. 'Which gives me an idea . . .'

Their nuptials were celebrated to a euphonious accompaniment by the pack. 'Something more to tell our children,' Marigold commented afterwards, before resuming her interrupted repose.

# Chapter Five

The day had passed in a whirl, inconsequent and unpredictable as a dream. The chief concern of Francis had merely been to get it over. But next morning, as he looked through a pile of letters the postman had brought, it struck him that something about it had been immensely odd. Mr Goodchild, his father's solicitor, had sent a wreath but had not come down himself, nor written explaining his absence.

The head partner of Goodchild, Morrow and Twigg was, of course, an extremely busy man. On the other hand, his firm had managed the Barraclough affairs for over a century. And Mr Goodchild was a stickler where form was involved, as well as a friend who often stayed at the Castle for shooting or fishing. It was surely to be expected that he would attend the funeral, and also that he would remain in the house after it, to deal with the family business. But he had done no such thing, made no sign apart from sending the flowers, nor was there a letter from him in the post today.

Francis had some idea that, on occasions like the present, family solicitors always appeared to open the Will and solemnly read it out. As apparently this was not so, he decided to get hold of the document himself: the Major, an orderly man, was sure to have a copy, and Francis guessed it would be in the strongbox, which was kept in a safe in the study.

On raising the lid of the box, the first thing he saw was a fat bundle of letters, all in his own writing. It seemed that every line he had ever sent home, from school, college, Paris, was lovingly collected here. Below that was another bundle, of his school reports, birth and christening certificates, and snapshots galore, of him as a baby, on his first pony, in his cricketing and football colours, his scholar's gown, on the steps of the Castle at his coming-of-age party, all with the description and date neatly written on the back.

Right at the bottom was a foolscap parchment with a

scribbled note, Last Will and Testament of A.G.B. It was roughly as Francis anticipated: various bequests to Army charities, kinsmen, friends and servants, and the bulk to him. There was a single codicil added later, leaving his medals and other military souvenirs to his cousin William, a little slap no doubt for his own refusal to join the Army, deserved perhaps but wounding all the same. But the document as a whole was straightforward and clear, raising no points that called for immediate attention. He would put it aside until the lawyer eventually felt disposed to communicate with him. For one thing, he was going to have his work cut out, acknowledging the scores of kind, regretful letters about his father's death; and then, he was too blissfully happy with Marigold to burden his mind with prosaic affairs.

To his mingled amusement and dismay, Marigold at once fell in love with the Castle, the village, the people and Ireland generally. Every aspect of them that he abhorred, she found entrancing. She browsed delightedly by the hour among the archives medals and swords, wandered through the great, austerely furnished rooms and explored the cellars, dragged him out to walk in the grounds and made him row her on the lake. City bred, she loved to hunt for newlaid eggs in the barns, pick apples and pears in the orchard, watch the hounds at their meals and try her hand at fishing. She marvelled at things she had always taken for granted, for instance, that doors and windows were never secured, even at night when there was no one at home.

'How you do trust the people here!' she exclaimed.

'Not round the corner!' was the laughing reply.

'But think of all the locking and fastening in Paris! And here, with all that wonderful silver and stuff! Anywhere else, it would all be gone.'

'Oh, no one would bother. They wouldn't know what to do with it. And somebody would be sure to see them. There are eyes in every hedge.'

But this form of national security was more than she could grasp. She maintained a fervent moonstruck belief in the local innocence. Direct proof that her confidence was misplaced had no effect whatever, even when her beautiful opal silk was found

32

in the wardrobe besmeared with Pepsicola and jam, and with a gaping tear in the skirt. Investigation by Francis revealed that one of the village troglodytes who helped in the kitchen had borrowed it for a dance, and thinking that mishaps so trifling would never be noticed, quietly put it back. Marigold was tickled to death.

'Just like the coloured people at home!' she crowed. 'Lovable and hopeless!'

'Hopeless, anyway.'

One thing grieved her, warm-hearted girl that she was, and that was what she took to be the local poverty. In particular, there was an old woman she often saw in the village store, buying screws of sugar or tea or a single turnip and hobbling wearily off with them to her cabin. Impulsively one day, Marigold bought a large assortment of good things and left them at the woman's door, thinking happily of the pleasure they would give. But when she told Francis of it, he was filled with consternation.

'Darling, why couldn't you ask me first?' he cried. 'You've no idea how touchy they are!'

'But Francis, she's so terribly poor.'

'Poor? With a widow's pension and three great sons on the dole! She doesn't like spending money, none of them do. It all goes under the mattress.'

'I never saw any sons around that place.'

'Much of the time they're in bed. The rest of it, in the pub.'

Shortly afterwards, a scowling man appeared at the Castle door with Marigold's bounty in his arms and thrust it at Maguire. 'The lady is after leavin' this behind her,' he snapped. 'She'll be wonderin' where it is.' And he stalked away without another word.

'Well, how do you like that!' Marigold cheerfully exclaimed when she heard about it.

'Not one little bit,' said Francis. Such things, he knew, could make enemies of them for the rest of their lives.

Thinking it over, he concluded his best plan would be to remove her from the locality before she had it all by the ears. Three weeks had passed and there was still no word from Mr Goodchild. He would, after all, approach him and seek his advice on various matters; and when this was obtained, they would return to Paris, as had always been their intention. They could come back now and again, if so inclined, whereas if they stayed here much longer, Marigold might not wish to leave at all. Accordingly, he wrote his letter and posted it off that very evening.

Mr Goodchild sat at his desk with the letter before him and dismally shook his head.

'Oh dear, dear, dear!' he muttered. 'A pretty kettle of fish!'

Sighing, he rang the bell for his clerk and, while he waited, looked through the missive again. He was of portly build and cherubic appearance, and as a human being kindly disposed to his fellow; but, as a legal man, he much disapproved of them all. There were the wealthy women who tried to manage their own affairs. There were the clients who brought him a lovely case, of the kind he enjoyed, then to reveal that they had thrown it away by rash correspondence. There were those who changed their mind every week, and those who never could make it up at all. There were others who never told him the truth until it was far too late. But the very worst of the lot, if he had to choose between them, was a certain type of legator.

A man with property to devise, be it great or small, should always – but here the entry of his clerk interrupted this familiar train of thought.

'Bring me the file of Arthur Gordon Barraclough, deceased,' he said. 'And open one for Mr Francis Hugh of that name.'

He should of course have dealt with this matter by now, but had continually put it off. The letter from Francis, however, made further delay impossible. The young man had found and read his father's Will – most improper! – and wanted some information. There were various bequests in cash that he would like to settle at once, but could not do so out of his income and, as Mr Goodchild knew, his capital was in Trust. He would like to know how far he might draw on family funds, pending Probate, and also to talk over certain matters connected with the property itself. As Mr Goodchild had possibly heard, he was newly married and, as soon as these few details were disposed of, wished to return to France. He would come up to

34

Dublin with pleasure, but his wife and he would be delighted if Mr Goodchild cared to spend a day or so with them in the country.

The clerk came in with the Barraclough files, one shabby and bulging, the other clean and flat.

'Thank you,' the lawyer said. 'Now please telephone to Castle Reef and tell Mr Francis – Mr Barraclough – that I will come down this afternoon, by car. Mr Morrow and Mr Twigg are in Court, I suppose? Then tell them for me, will you? I shall be back in a couple of days.'

A trip out of town was highly inconvenient at this moment, but he felt it his duty to make it. It was a mark of proper respect to young Francis, who was now his client, no longer a client's son. And what he had to say might come more easily there in the Castle than over a desk in a Dublin office. There or here, however, he was not looking forward to the task ahead. A man with property to bequeath . . . As he drove along the country roads, his often stated views on the point ran through his mind again and again.

It was pleasant to meet young Francis after so long, although the occasion was overshadowed by the Major himself being gone, so prematurely, so contrary to what should have been, which only proved once more . . .

'I am sorry my wife is out,' said Francis. 'You must excuse her, she is photographing some tinkers. In any case, we shall have to talk business, shan't we? But first let us have some tea.'

'Just a cup, just a cup,' said Mr Goodchild nervously. He refused muffins and sandwiches and, hastily swallowing a drop or two, pushed the cup itself away. Then, drawing a deep breath, he began: 'Francis, I refer to your letter of yesterday's date. There is no use beating about the bush. I am sorry to say the Will you found is invalid. Your father made a new one, in April of last year.'

'No, did he?' said Francis in surprise. 'He never breathed a word about it to me. Has he cut me off with a shilling?'

'Not so, by any means. But what he has done is very strange indeed. He did it on the natural assumption that he would live many more years. Such a mistake! A man with property to bequeath should always do so bearing in mind that he may

35

be dead tomorrow. I mean by that, he should leave things as he really, finally, wants them left. Not with a view to their disposition having an effect which, however desirable, would depend for its success on circumstances which may have completely altered.'

'This is really most alarming,' Francis said, trying not to sound as if he meant it. 'What disposition has he made, and what effect did he hope it would have?'

'Your father felt – he opened his mind to me freely – that you did not value your inheritance as you should. He felt you had no interest in it, merely taking it for granted that it would eventually fall into your lap. You know, of course how much the place and the traditions of his family had always meant to him. He thought you needed a shock – that was the expression he used to me, over and over again. Against all my advice, in spite of anything that I could say, therefore he took the extraordinary step of leaving the place away from you, to another party, with, however, reversion to you or your heirs when that party should also decease. The party was of much the same age, might for that matter have predeceased him, at any rate in the normal way would have enjoyed the bequest for a very few years. The intent was not to deprive you, rather, to cause you to reflect.'

'Well! As you say, very strange indeed. I had absolutely no idea.' It could have been a great deal worse. He was back where he was, next in line, which would save him no end of fuss and worry in the immediate future. Marigold and he could be off to France tomorrow! But there was pain in it, nevertheless. 'You have only heard my father's side of it, Mr Goodchild,' he said somewhat bitterly. 'This house is a museum, what with the medals, swords, uniforms, letters and diaries about battles and wounds and promotions. All as dead as the Dodo. I wanted to paddle my own canoe and see some life before I had to sink into it. When I got the scholarship to Magdalen, my father's only thought was of how it might affect my career in the Army. I told him then I would not be a soldier, and he was very decent about it. As about everything, always. But when I got my Double First and hoped he would feel proud, he only said that I must have been overworking and needed a good long rest at home. It upset him awfully when I moved to Paris, he couldn't understand it. But he could never understand me at all. When I came of age, he asked what I wanted – I could have anything, a super car, a yacht, a racehorse or two! I was just between Harrow and Magdalen, and I asked him to give me the smaller library for my own, to work in, and to let me do it up myself, move all that dreary old lumber out. He was shattered at the very idea, as if I were a vandal. Oh! excuse me for running on like this, but I have had my troubles too.'

'To be sure, to be sure, father and son,' the lawyer agreed. 'And it was not simply a matter of age. The world is changing so very fast, as you of course realised, but your father did not. It often happens in old, distinguished families like his.'

Francis forced a laugh. 'I have sometimes envied the Americans poking about in the ancient graveyard here, looking for a grandpapa or mamma, nothing further back . . . Well, to business. I suppose the place is left to his cousin Bill? He is nearest, after me.'

'Well,' said Mr Goodchild slowly, and paused. He had told but a half of his tale and the worst was yet to come. 'No. Not to General Sir William Barraclough. It does not go to one of the name at all. He has left it – and Francis, again I will stress, I did all in my power to dissuade him, going further perhaps than a mere advisor should – to a man formerly of his regiment and afterwards in his service. To Patrick Kevin Maguire.'

'*Maguire!*' shouted Francis. 'You can't be serious!'

'I am sorry indeed.'

'But Maguire is our butler!'

'Was,' said Mr Goodchild, in a sepulchral tone. 'He is now the owner of Castle Reef, to use and enjoy in his lifetime, rents and produce likewise accrueing to him. He may not alter, demolish or construct, nor dispose of any furnishings, fitments, or paraphernalia, but otherwise he has full possession.'

'My father must have been mad! Surely you thought he was mad?'

'Humanly speaking, yes. Never a week goes by but one of my clients does something which, humanly speaking, I would consider insane. But mad in the legal sense, no. Your father

**37**

knew exactly what he was doing. His mind was as clear as a bell.'

'Then there's no contesting this?'

'There are no grounds whatever on which we could do so. The property is not entailed. You will of course remember how Piers Barraclough fell out with his only son, Thomas, and left the place to a Mrs Bruggle? But happily father and son were reconciled, and that Will was revoked almost at once.'

Francis had no recollection of this family disagreement, which had taken place in 1824.

'But what a position to put me in' he cried. 'Did he not consider my feelings at all?'

'He did, indeed, very much so. As I have already told you, he was anxious to give you a shock.'

'Well, he has done it. Here am I, in my own family place, the guest of my own butler.'

'What sort of man is Maguire?' asked Mr Goodchild. 'Much will depend on that. I have seen him, of course, when staying here, but have had no dealings with him.'

'Oh, the typical excellent wooden-faced Army servant. Orderly, efficient, honest. Devoted to my father, and my father to him. And devoted to the family tradition as well. I imagine he will be as shocked as I am. Perhaps he will even refuse the legacy. I suppose he could?'

'Yes, but I should be greatly surprised. I have never known anyone to renounce a windfall of this description. And he has no further need to play the exemplary servant. I fear, Francis, that you will have to make the best of it. You are still the heir, and likely to inherit at about the time of life that you would have expected. And there are substantial monies and assets, other than those of the estate itself, which come directly to you.'

'The family jewels!' Francis burst out. 'I want to give them to Marigold. And I don't even know where they are.'

'Nor I. If lodged in the Bank, they are yours. But if they are in the house, I am afraid they pass with the other effects to Maguire.'

'They were not in the strong-box. There was nothing there but the Will and . . . and a lot of old papers.'

'We should not build too much on that. Your father had little

38

idea as to value. He was perfectly capable of keeping the jewels in some open drawer.'

'Maguire will look sweet in my mother's tiara !'

'Now, let us not cross our bridges before we come to them. He cannot dispose of the jewels, nor have them reset.'

'I daresay. But I should have liked to see them on my wife before she was middle-aged.'

'My dear boy,' the lawyer groaned, 'I can only repeat what I have said before. Every argument I could think of, all such powers of persuasion as I possess, were used in the endeavour to change your father's mind.' He leaned wearily back in his chair, and the two of them were silent for a while. Then, 'Francis,' said Mr Goodchild plaintively, 'I wonder if I might ask you to give me a drink? This has rather taken it out of me.'

'Of course, I'm sorry, rotten host . . .' Francis ran to the bell and gave it a vigorous push. 'Oh my stars !' he then exclaimed, 'I have sent for the Guv'nor !'

'Sir !' said the potentate, quietly appearing.

'Would you mind bringing some drinks, please, Maguire? What will you have Mr Goodchild?'

'Brandy, if possible, thank you.'

'Of course. And Maguire, by the way, which room is Mr Goodchild in?'

'Gallipoli, sir. I have taken his things up.' And the lord of the Castle withdrew, as softly as he had come.

# Chapter Six

While Mr Goodchild recruited his strength with the brandy, Francis hurried away in search of his wife. He had insisted that the news be withheld from Maguire until it was known to her, for he imagined that she would be greatly distressed. The lawyer had demurred, on the grounds that a chief beneficiary ought not to be left in the dark for even a short space of time. Francis had warmly pointed out that everybody concerned had been left in the dark for over three weeks. Mr Goodchild owned himself in the wrong, saying he had liked his duty so little that he had postponed it from day to day. Nevertheless, he pleaded, he had tried to make amends, both by coming down here in person and by the irregularity of his procedure, since, properly, Maguire and not Francis should have been notified first; but the very idea of that provoked such a storm that he judged it wiser to yield.

Marigold had returned from the tinkers' camp and was run to earth in the barn, photographing a donkey foal.

'I never saw anything so cute in my life,' she said. 'All cotton wool and great black eyes. Would the mother mind you picking him up? I'd love to take the two of you together.'

'Do you know what that father of mine has done?'

'Why no, how could I, unless you tell me?' she replied, focusing her camera again. 'Just keep it, though, until I get this shot.'

Francis took the foal in his arms with an air of bitter patience, and dropped it as soon as the camera clicked.

'Now! What's biting you?'

'He has left the bloody place to Maguire!'

'What, the Castle?'

'Lock, stock and barrel.'

Marigold digested the information with unruffled calm. 'I

40

think that was very sweet of him,' she observed presently.

'Sweet!'

'Well, he knew you didn't want it. So he gives it to Old Faithful. Something like it happened back home, long ago. It was one of the tales my grandmother loved to tell. Son wouldn't bother with plantation, planter left it to a darky he was fond of. Only trouble was, darky went to the dogs.'

'Plantations, dahkies, dem quaint ole tahmes in the deep South, is that all you have to say? The whole affair is grotesque, outrageous. And who says I didn't want the place?' He suddenly began to feel that he wanted it like blazes. 'Our old family estate, handed over to a menial! What on earth will he do with it?'

'Sell it, maybe.'

'He can't do that. It has to revert to me. My father has played a stupid practical joke. His idea, Goodchild says, was to give me a shock because he thought I took no interest in the estate affairs. So he left it to Maguire for his life only, assuming that they would pop off at about the same time. I never heard anything so crazy. And Goodchild agrees.'

'People are crazy,' said Marigold, placidly. 'Your Mr Goodchild should know it by now.'

'Well, come on up to the house and meet him, do. I suppose you are still the châtelaine until Maguire turns us out.'

'O.K., O.K. Just let me take one more shot of this little honey and I'll be along.'

'You seem to have no sense of proportion whatever.' And he stumped away, feeling angry with her for the very first time since they had met.

Why, thought Marigold, had *she* no sense of proportion because Francis was in a tizzy about his father's Will? As long as he believed himself the heir, he had fretted and fumed; and here he was, fretting and fuming again. There was, she knew, no rhyme or reason in family matters and she had never really attempted to fathom his. She did hope, however, that he was not turning into a husband already.

On the eve of her wedding her mother had warned her that, while men might vary, husbands were all alike. But for her grasp of this truth, she said, she would have landed up in the

41

divorce court, like everyone else. Bear in mind, she added, that when a husband gets upset, whatever a wife may do or say is bound to be wrong. These were not the words of a critical mother-in-law to be, for she had taken to Francis at once and wholly approved of the match. But this gulf between men and husbands, similar to that which Mr Goodchild saw between human beings and clients, was a fact of life she thought every young bride should know.

Having taken her photo and fondled the little ass a while longer, Marigold reluctantly tore herself away and went back to the house. Francis and the lawyer were in the library, arguing it seemed, and she decided to dress before she joined them. In honour of Mr Goodchild, a few people had been asked to dine, and she wanted to appear at her best, so that Francis could take pride in her looks, whatever her mental failings might be.

In their bedroom she found Maguire, turning back the sheets and laying their night clothes out. He explained that Mrs Jeffars had the evening off, and that, since he would have to clear up singlehanded after dinner, he had taken the liberty of preparing things now. There was absolutely no change in his demeanour. In her forthcoming way Marigold made him a pleasant little speech, suited to the occasion, the results of which, after he had withdrawn, caused her to roll on the bed in fits of laughter. Presently, having somewhat recovered, she put on her gold brocade and went downstairs.

Mr Goodchild and Francis rose to their feet as she came in, the former looking at her with startled admiration. Evidently like all the others, he had expected something else.

'I'm sorry I wasn't there when you arrived,' Marigold said, shaking hands. 'But I knew you had business to settle with Francis. Now I hope we can all relax.'

'I hope so, I hope so,' he mumbled, bemusedly retaining her hand in his. 'I am delighted to meet you, Mrs Barraclough, delighted. Bless my soul! Yes, indeed, delighted.'

'But you will have to call me Marigold, won't you?' she asked, smiling and gently freeing her hand from his grasp. 'Well, what stage have we got to?'

'Mr Goodchild wants to see Maguire at once,' said Francis

wearily. 'My own idea, is to get this dinner over first. Had I known what was going to happen I should never have fixed it up.'

'Francis, I really deem it incumbent on me . . .' Mr Goodchild began.

'But what do you want to see him for?' Marigold asked. 'He is very busy. Mrs Jeffars is out.'

'Why, to inform him without further delay of this . . . this . . .'

'Oh that!' said Marigold, laughing. 'Don't worry. He knows.'

'He knows!' cried Francis. 'How does he know? Did you tell him?'

'Well, I had to say something. He was upstairs, turning the bed down like nothing was altered. I congratulated him, and he didn't know what in the world I was talking about. So what could I do but explain?'

'And what did he say?'

Marigold went off into peals of laughter. 'Nothing much, that I recall. 'Very good, madam,' or something. Oh stop, yes, Francis, he wants to ask you about the wine for dinner.'

'Wine! Dinner! Does he mean to wait on us?'

'I gather he does.'

'He can't be human,' Francis declared impatiently.

'I shouldn't bank on that,' said Mr Goodchild, his legal instincts reviving. 'The surprise will have been very great. It may require time before the fact sinks in. However, our immediate problem is disposed of. Francis, if you will kindly show me the way to my room, I think I shall dress for dinner. You will excuse me, Maria?'

'Marigold.'

'Marigold, Marigold, to be sure. I beg your pardon. This has been a most confusing day.'

Francis conducted him to Gallipoli, so named because a picture of the battle there covered most of one wall. The bed was neatly turned back, Mr Goodchild's striped pyjamas lay on the eiderdown, his slippers stood on the floor beneath, his evening clothes and dressing-gown hung in the wardrobe, his hairbrushes, stud-box, ties and spongebag were all in their

43

rightful places. Beside the washstand was a great brass pitcher with a towel across the top, for running hot water in bedrooms had not reached the Castle as yet.

Having installed his guest, Francis went to find Maguire, who was putting a few last touches to the table in the dining-room.

'It is very good of you to do all this and I appreciate it,' he said. 'Tomorrow we must have a talk, but I am more than grateful for your help tonight.'

'Sir. About the wine for the first course, sir, smoked trout. The Moselle is all drunk, but we have Chablis and Sancerre.'

'Oh either one, whichever you like. And thanks very much.' He hardly thought he could be awake. 'You're perfectly right,' he said to Marigold, 'he's just the same as ever. Yes, sir, no, sir. Darling, you look gorgeous. I'm sorry I was so nasty. It just seems to be one confounded thing after the other these days.'

Marigold gave him a kiss. 'Let's take it easy,' she said. 'We've got each other, we're young and well, not exactly half-witted, and we don't have money problems. It could be a whole lot worse!'

'You're wonderful! How I wish these awful people weren't coming and we could go to bed!'

'And bay the moon!' This, since the musical interlude with the hounds, was their code-word for making love.

But coming the awful people were, and soon they began to arrive. Francis had chosen the guests with care: his father's dinners were always successful and he meant to show what he could do in that line himself. As it happened, however, his choice could not have been more unfortunate. He had been away too long to remember, if he had ever known, the ins and outs of the locality. Colonel Beaulieu thought the Rector a silly old ass, and the Rector disapproved, as far as disapproval was in him, of hunting. For reasons which both had long forgotten, their wives were at daggers drawn. A local solicitor, Mr Quirke, specially asked for Mr Goodchild, was the unluckiest dip of all. Mr Goodchild knew the type and loathed it and, aware of the reason for his presence, was much affronted. Mr Quirke resented Mr Goodchild; he had always wanted the Barra-clough business and put his failure to get it down to anti-republican prejudice. Colonel Beaulieu could not for the life of him think, as his manner made clear, what Quirke was doing in a gentleman's house; and even the Rector was 'just a little surprised' to see him there.

Happily, the weather just then was beautiful, a real Indian summer, and they could discuss it exhaustively over their drinks until Maguire sounded the gong.

At dinner Marigold had the Rector on her right and the Colonel on her left, Francis had their wives the other way round to avoid any signs of preference, and the two solicitors faced each other across the table in between.

'How I do envy you that man!' said Mrs Beaulieu, when Maguire had served them and left the room. 'Impossible to find a real butler these days. Either they drink, or join in the conversation at table, or stand the wine in hot water, to take the chill off.'

'Really? I'm not in the butler class,' said Mr Quirk with a light laugh, intended to show how entirely he felt at his ease.

As statements of the obvious usually are, the remark was followed by silence. It was broken by Marigold, observing that Maguire was a peach.

'And highly intelligent, too,' beamed the Rector. 'We had a most interesting talk about Africa, only the other day. He is all for black majority rule, one man, one vote.'

'Then he wants his head examined,' growled the Colonel.

'He never talks to me,' said Francis hurriedly. 'About Africa or anything else. It was different with my father. They were as thick as could be.'

'Natural enough, when he saved your father's life,' said Mr Quirke.

'I think my father saved his, though, didn't he?'

'Correct,' said the Colonel. 'Battle of the Bulge.'

'That's not what I hear,' said Mr Quirke.

'Can't help what you hear,' snorted the Colonel. 'I was there. And Major Barraclough was mentioned in despatches for it, not for the first time either.'

The formal reference to 'Major Barraclough' was not thrown away on Mr Quirke. 'But they always gave officers the

45

credit, didn't they?' he sneered. 'All the medals, and that class of tripe?'

There was another longer silence, and the Colonel's face grew slowly purple.

'War is a terrible thing, a terrible thing,' moaned the Rector. 'I wonder, shall we ever rise above it?'

'No,' said the Colonel.

'Not while there's money in it, eh?' said Mr Quirke, with an air of jovial agreement.

At this moment Maguire came in to change the dishes, forcing a truce. Marigold began to recount her amusing time with the tinkers that afternoon, thinking she had never met such a goddam prickly crowd in her life.

'Tinkers!' said Mr Quirke, who somehow felt inspired to lead the conversation. 'You have to call them itinerants, Marigold, now.' A quiver went round the table at this use of her Christian name. 'That's Lord Carrageen's land they're squatting on. He has asked me to get them off. I told him, he hasn't a chance in hell. What do you say, Goodchild?'

'I have no opinion to offer, Mr Quirke.

'Ah, now, we're all friends here,' said Mr Quirke unabashed. 'I'm the last one to blether about me client's affairs, but it's just between these four walls. Trouble is, some of the county council fellows were thrashed by the old Lord's bailiff when they were boys, for stealing and that, and they haven't forgotten. And Carrageen's an awkward customer too. He has four actions coming along, one of them with the Convent itself! Suits me fine, but he's going to lose the lot.'

'What an interesting life you must have, Mr Quirke,' said Marigold brightly.

'Most,' said Mr Goodchild.

'The name is Aloysius,' said Mr Quirke. 'Looshie to you!' and he raised his glass to her in courtly style.

This practically put an end to speech for the rest of the meal. With the two women in the drawing-room afterwards, Marigold did extremely well and soon they were chatting away, almost as if they could bear the sight of each other. But darkness fell again the instant the men came in, four of them with faces of thunder, the irrepressible Mr Quirke demanding, be-

46

fore he even sat down, a drop of Scotch. Francis had to go and look for it, as Maguire by now had disappeared. The Rector never drank, and the others declined to do so in their present company. It was like spending an evening in a snake pit, Marigold reckoned, and she wondered if social life in Ireland were all of this pattern. At times the only sound to be heard was the grim ticking of a grandfather clock at the far end of the room.

The guests took their leave at the earliest moment that bare politeness would allow. Mr Quirke was disposed to linger, but was thwarted by Francis, waiting for him to follow the rest in a manner that was not to be mistaken. Having exchanged brief chilly good-nights and received their hollow thanks, he returned to the others and sank, exhausted, on to a sofa.

'Oh mercy,' he said. 'Don't hold it against me, Mr Goodchild. I never met Quirke before, but he's supposed to be the leading lawyer round here.'

'I don't doubt it for an instant,' Mr Goodchild said drily. 'It is what we are getting these days. Cattle dealers' sons. They pass their examinations all right, but have no ethical standards of any description.'

'I think he was just a bit nervous,' Marigold said.

'Then I should be sorry to meet him at the top of his form.'

'Well, let us all have a night-cap,' said Francis pacifically. 'There is one comfort – nothing else can happen now !'

At this moment a car came up the drive at speed and stopped with a screech of brakes outside. Someone knocked loudly on the door several times, and the deep voice of Juno was lifted in displeasure. There was a short interval, and the visitor pounded again, in a still more peremptory manner.

'I'd better go,' said Francis. 'Maguire mustn't be back yet. Callers, at this time of night !'

He opened the front door, to find a squad car halted on the drive and three embarrassed Guards waiting on the step.

'I'm sorry indeed to break in like this, Mr Francis,' said the Sergeant, 'But I was telephoning some little while and I couldn't raise you. I greatly regret your father's death, sir,' he added, removing his cap. His companions muttered agreement and took theirs off as well.

'I know you do,' said Francis, in the prescribed form. Surely

47

they haven't come to say that? he wondered crossly.

'Could I just have a word or two with you, sir? Quiet like?'

'Certainly, come in. We'll go to the library.'

The guards, breathing heavily, sat down with the caps on their knees, the two underlings with their eyes turned up to the ceiling, the Sergeant staring round the bookshelves, as if looking to them for assistance.

'There was a little bit of crossness at Flanagan's, Mr Francis,' he began, feeling his way. 'Some of the boys had drink taken, you know how they are. The long and the short of it was, Flanagan called us in, and there was nothing for it, we had to take your man Maguire to the barracks.'

'*Maguire?*' asked Francis, in stupefaction. 'Drinking at Flanagan's?' I never knew he went there.'

'Nor he don't, not regular. But when the fit is on him, he do make an evening of it. And the lads like to see him, he's great for telling a story when he's had a few jars. Ah, he's a genius!'

'Stories? Maguire? What sort of stories?'

'One thing or another, he has a whole repertoire. Well, to-night, it was how he saved your father's life, under a hail of bullets. That's a favourite with the public always. But now he was embroidering on it and it seems, he pushed it too far. Told them all your father had left the Castle to him, in consideration of his gallantry. They thought that was too fanciful altogether. They wanted the usual, about torturing suspects in Belfast, or the British officers driving the Irish lads into battle before them at revolver point, themselves cowering behind, or tying the Cyprus people to guns and blowing them off, honest-to-god stuff that they could believe. But no, Maguire would stick by it, the Castle was his, and the end of the story was, Denis Mangan called him a liar and all hell broke loose.'

'Damage!' croaked one of the others.

'Broken windows! Blood!' the second chimed in.

'So Flanagan phoned us, and what could we do, only pull Maguire in?' asked the Sergeant, on a note of appeal.

'What indeed?' asked Francis, his mind reeling.

'We had a party with him all right, the three of us. And the language! He'll have cooled off be the morning, but, sir, I'm afraid we must bring a charge. Flanagan himself got a belt on the poll that stretched him, lifeless, for half an hour. And there's a crowd of witnesses to it.'

'God Almighty!'

' 'Twill have been the grief of losing the Major, sir, that clouded his judgement,' said the Sergeant kindly. 'Still and all, we have our job to do.'

'Well, Sergeant, now wait a minute,' said Francis slowly. 'I had no idea that Maguire's imagination was so active! But part of his story is true.'

'Well yes, Mr Francis, no one ever doubted a single blessed word he spoke before. And they admired him no end for saving your father's life, at the risk of his own. But people don't like to be made fools of, sir, and asked to swallow a tale of cock and bull. It was that, and the drink of course, that set them off.'

'We are talking at cross purposes, I'm afraid,' Francis said. 'The tale of cock and bull was saving my father's life. It was my father who saved him. But never mind that. It is a fact that my father has left him the Castle. I only knew it myself today, or it would have been announced before.'

The Guards all gaped at him, as if fearing he might be drunk as well.

'Left him the Castle, sir?' asked the Sergeant, in a strangled tone.

'Left him the Castle.'

'Jesus, Mary and Joseph!' The Sergeant took out a handkerchief and dazedly wiped his brow. 'And him in the lock-up! We can't have that. We'll hurry on down and bring him up here. I hope he'll not be too hard on us, sure, what could we do? Would you ever put in a word, sir, if he's fractious at all?'

'I think he had better stay where he is for tonight,' Francis said. 'I'll come first thing in the morning and pick him up myself.'

'Oh sir, no, that would never do, he could bring an action against us,' the Sergeant cried in agony. 'We haven't a leg to stand on. The landlord of Castle Reef in the cells, only for claiming his right! He'll put Mr Quirke on us, that'll be what! And I'm only a couple of years off the pinsion!'

'But what about the damage he's done?'

'Oh that, there'll be no more about that, if anyone tries to make something of that, we'll quinch him!'

'Very well so,' said Francis, marvelling, not for the first time, at the flexibility of Irish procedure. 'I'll come along with you, shall I?'

'If you will, Mr Francis, sir, sure, you're much too good.'

'Right, hang on a moment. I'll just tell my wife and we'll be going.'

He returned to the drawing-room and gave a précis of the evening's events to Marigold and the lawyer. Neither was anywhere near as astounded as he had been: Mr Goodchild apparently was confirmed in some view he had held all along and Marigold was simply amused.

'I knew he couldn't really be like he seemed,' she chuckled.

'Split personality, typical,' said Mr Goodchild, with quiet satisfaction. 'They are all the same, nothing to choose between them. The illusion we must all overcome is, that there are any exceptions whatsoever.'

'And I thought you said that nothing else could happen now!' Marigold went off into peals of laughter.

'I'll never say such a thing again, as long as I live!' And, leaving them to digest and enjoy the news, he rejoined the Guards and set off on his hazardous errand.

# Chapter Seven

Maguire woke up like a man coming round from an anaesthetic. There was a singing in his ears, and a buzzing in his head as if bees were swarming there. His body seemed to fly up and down, as if tossed in a blanket. He could not even guess where he was, but shrank from opening his eyes. The warmth of the air and the light that shone through his lids meant that it was a fine sunny day, and none too early. More than that he could not feel sure of, and he lay quietly as he was until his mind should begin to function.

Presently, blurred fragments of the evening before came drifting back. He had gone to the pub and made a night of it, had been as usual the life and soul of the party. But, also as usual, of what had occurred after a certain point was reached, he could remember nothing. It was wrapped in oblivion. Cautiously, he opened an eye and found himself in his room, on his bed, partly undressed. How had he got there? On the bedside table someone had left a carafe of water and a mug, as in former happier days the Major did when he came back under the weather, giving him a hand and never speaking of it again, like the gentleman he was. But the Major was gone.

With an effort, he opened his other eye, and now he saw a note beside the carafe. 'Don't stir till you feel inclined,' it ran. 'Mr Goodchild had to return to Dublin, so there is no rush at all. And don't worry about the rest, we have sorted it out between us. F. B.' It must be from Mr Francis. Mr Francis had put him to bed, and very decent too, his father all over again. But what did he, Maguire, care if Mr Goodchild stayed or went, why was he not to worry, what had there been to sort out? Puzzled, he went through the note again, moving his lips as he read.

Blimey! The Castle. The Major had left him the Castle. That was it. He had gone to Flanagan's to celebrate. He had drunk and made merry with the lads until he passed out. One

51

of them would have run him home. So, up to a point, the note made sense. Of course Mr Goodchild would have to see him, most likely had come for the purpose. But what did Mr Francis mean by 'the rest'?

Painfully, he got up and went to the basin to plunge his head in cold water. Glancing up at the shaving-mirror, he was appalled to see that both his eyes were black. More must have happened than he could recollect, it must be, he had knocked against something or tumbled over, demeaned himself in some way, let the family down. Probably, in his new position, it was beneath him to enter the pub at all.

He shaved with care, put on his Sunday suit, polished his boots until they shone, and went downstairs. Francis and Marigold had gone for a walk and there seemed to be no one about. But as he reached the hall, the strident notes of a popular song beat on his ear and made him wince. They were here again, were they, those trippers from town, enticed by the lovely warm weather? For some years past, the common people had taken to treating the Castle grounds as their own, driving up in their Minis, shattering the peace with their transistors, bringing their food and littering the place with bottles and bags. The Major in his easy way – soft, Maguire had always considered it – would take no notice. It was the spirit of the time, he said, there was no such thing as private property now. If you asked them to leave, they would simply refuse, and then there was nothing more to be done. Oh, wasn't there, though? Maguire had often thought.

Guided by the radio's howl, he made his way to the west end of the house and peered through a window. Yes, there they were, by the edge of the lake – on his land, without so much as a by-your-leave! Four of them, a fat slob of a man leaning against a scarlet Cortina and sucking a bottle, while three women, one with her hair in curlers, were unwrapping refreshments, and laying them out on the grass.

Maguire marched out to confront the intruders, his face at its most wooden, his stride unhurried but martial.

'Now then, you,' he said. 'This is a private park.'

'No, is that right?' said the man cheerfully. He wore a cotton T-shirt stamped *Never Say Die*, with a bush of fur peeping out of the front. 'I'd have taken me oath it was commonage.'

The women cackled in appreciation of this rejoinder.

'I must ask you to leave,' Maguire continued, without raising his voice.

'No harm in asking,' the man replied, taking a pull at his bottle of stout. 'Would there be any offence, if I asked who you were? You look like one of them giant pandas.'

The squeals of delight which hailed this sally all but drowned the transistor.

'You have five minutes to be gone,' said Maguire curtly, and turned on his heel.

'Sorry, me lord, I left me watch at home!' the man bawled after him, to a fresh outbreak of ear-splitting mirth. With that, noisily laughing, the four sat down on the grass and began their meal.

When he reached the house, Maguire turned to face them and composedly took out his watch. After exactly five minutes he went indoors, to yells of triumph from the party, who took it as a retreat. A few seconds later he reappeared, with an enormous Irish wolfhound bitch that pelted down the slope towards them, barking as she came. Like most of that breed, she was of an amiable disposition, and she had nothing in mind but a friendly social call. But when the strangers leaped up in terror, the man shouting, the woman screaming, she saw her mistake. Good people were never afraid of dogs. With fierce growls and sudden rushes, her lips drawn back from her teeth, she herded them into their car and flew after it, vociferating, as it roared away down the drive. That duty done, she hastened back to the picinic spread and, after gobbling up the sausage rolls, fell to work on the roasted chicken.

No bloody guts, mused Maguire, who had followed the operation with the critical eye of a brigadier. What did he always tell the Major? only the poor good man would never mind him.

'Here, Juno, that's the girl,' he shouted. 'Walks!'

Juno bounded joyfully back, a drumstick protruding from her jaws, and the pair of them set off together. The fresh air and his victory over the slobs had much restored Maguire; and now, as he went the way he always took with the dog, through the shrubbery, beside the river as far as the waterfall, then into the wood, along the bridle paths where the Major and he so often rode, he began to feel quite bobbish again.

The wood ended abruptly and, passing from its shadow into the sun, he had a fine view of the whole Castle. It was known as such, being built on the site of a mediaeval stronghold, but in fact was a Palladian house, the work of a foreign architect, one of the best of that time. The name derived from a dreaded reef in the sea which bounded the lands to the west, lands so broad that the sea itself was but a vague and distant shimmer: only a great wooden hulk, wrecked there long ago and never salvaged, stood up against the skyline to mark its presence. This hulk, picturesque and beloved of tourists, had always been an irritation to Maguire's orderly soul: just like 'em, leaving it to lie about forever, the way they left piles of stones all over the shop, buildings that had tumbled down, lazy showers, never cleared nothing up. He'd do something about it himself, see if he didn't, now he was in charge.

Yes, everything in sight belonged to him, here where he had served and fetched and carried. When the young lady broke it to him he had been stunned by the news, unable to grasp it. He had gone about his usual chores in the house like a machine. But now, with his brain clear and working well, he began to feel it was no more than his due. It was the reward for years of selfless devotion. And the Major had seen him as the right man to take it on, his hands as the fitting ones in which to leave it. That was what Mr Francis got for swanning about in Paris. There was justice in life after all.

'Come on, Juno, let's go home.' It was time for a little drink.

An hour later, Francis and Marigold returned from their walk, having discussed the affair from end to end. They were in the peaceful frame of mind which follows when a course of action is decided. This was, to pack up and go at once, the position here being beyond them. Mr Goodchild had freely confessed that it was all beyond him too. Saddened by the task which had brought him down, all but destroyed by the frightful dinner and finished off by the unseemly events at the pub, he had told them Maguire should be left in the younger, stronger hands of Mr Twigg. In the whole dire gallery of his clients, there had been nothing like him before; and, after handing Francis a duplicate of the Will for the wretch's perusal, he had taken an early departure.

Francis had then called on Flanagan, who was swathed in bandages and using a crutch. Despite the promise of immunity made by the Guards, he had compensated him for his wounds and the wreckage. Nothing as yet was generally known of the legacy, the Guards having promised to treat it as confidential. An announcement would have to be made, but Maguire could make it himself in his own good time. He would hardly be well enough to do so, Francis reckoned, before Marigold and he were out of the country. Marigold thought it a pity they had to miss all the fun, but Francis replied he had had as much fun as he could bear, and any more would prove fatal.

But as they walked happily through the hall, hand in hand, Mrs Jeffars popped out from behind a suit of armour, where she had been lying in wait. Fearfully, she gave it as her opinion that Maguire was bewitched. He had sat himself down in the drawing-room, you'd say he owned it, and was going on with the Major's whisky. She had never passed any remarks before but he always did take liberties, respectably though, out of sight. Now there he was, a-lolling and a-drinking in the Major's armchair, with his two eyes black on him, enough to frighten the crows, and for the whole blessed world to see!

'Guess I'll start packing right away,' said Marigold under her breath.

'And do it fast!' he murmured back.

'Never mind Maguire, Mrs Jeffars, come into the library a moment,' he said, opening the door for her. 'Please sit down, I have something to tell you. You were out last night, or I would have done it before. I didn't know, until Mr Goodchild came, what were the terms of my father's Will.'

'God rest and reward him!' she intoned, eagerly pricking her ears up.

'Needless to say, you were not forgotten. He has left you two thousand pounds.'

'He was always the best in the world!' cried Mrs Jeffars, clasping her hands. She had given the matter a good deal of thought, and was expecting five hundred at most.

'Then as regards your employment. If you were still in his service when he died, and chose to stay on with his heir, that would be between the two of you. But, whenever you left and whatever the reason, the estate was to pay you the pension he always promised.'

'Of course I'll stay with you and Mrs Marigold, then,' she cried, staring. 'Sure, why wouldn't I?'

'But my wife and I are returning to France, immediately.'

'Not for ever, though? God forbid it!'

'I think, for a considerable time.' But the hurt bewildered look on her face was too much for him altogether. 'I had better tell you the truth, Mrs Jeffars.' And tell it he did. 'But do please keep it to yourself until we have gone.'

'The Lord save us! the poor decent Major . . . But he never did know the half that fellow had in his mind. So that's why your man is in there, a-preening himself like a duke! Oh, I'll be out of this tomorrow, sure as the rain. I'll take me pension and go. I've always worked for gentry and always will. And the gerrls will tell you the same, and the outside men. There'll not be a soul left in the place . . .' She rocked to and fro in her chair, the lamentations pouring like a burn in spate. 'And what of yourself, then, Mr Francis? What kind of a trick was that, that he would play it on you?'

'Well, he had his reasons, but never mind them now. And I am still the heir. Maguire has it only for life.'

'And won't he live for ever, if only to spite you?' Now she remembered something that the impudence of Maguire had pushed to the back of her mind. 'Oh, Mr Francis, the Sergeant was on, and please will you ring him back as soon as you can? He said, how 'twas very urgent.'

'Oh, hell!' important things last, as usual. 'All right, thank you!'

He assumed that further claims in respect of the night before were flowing in. Mr Flanagan had stung him nicely and, no doubt, the joyful tidings had spread. But it turned out to be a different case altogether. A wellknown and much respected citizen of Ballinaduff, the county town, had taken a little bit of a drive in the Park with his wife and two other ladies. There was no harm at all, it was only what everyone did, and the

Major had never objected. They got out of the car for a moment, to admire the lake and the view, when some ignorant fellow came up and ordered them off. But before they had time to leave, he set a great savage murderous brute of a dog at them, the size of a calf. All were severely bitten and the gentleman's wife, who was expecting, had to be treated for shock.

'But there is no savage dog here,' said Francis. 'There's only Juno, and she wouldn't hurt a fly. And who can have ordered them off?'

The Sergeant coughed. 'From the description we got, sir, I'm thinking 'twas Mr Maguire.'

'Let Maguire deal with it, then. Where do I come in?'

'We thought it best to speak to you, Mr Francis, because the gentleman insists the dog be destroyed. That's why he came to us. The other matters, he is taking to Mr Quirke.'

'Juno destroyed? Over my dead body! Who is this idiot?'

'Denis Halloran, sir, a national teacher. With friends in politics,' the Sergeant groaned.

'I'll ask Dr McLeod to look at these bites, to begin with.'

'Ah, he'd never see Dr McLeod. Dr McLeod is Fine Gael, Mr Francis, and Denis Halloran is Fianna Fail.'

'Fine Gael, Fianna Fail, Bedlam,' Francis roared, boiling over. 'Leave it to me, Sergeant. But understand this – if anyone lays a finger on Juno, I'll shoot him myself.'

Slamming down the receiver, he rushed to the drawing room and burst in with the force of a gale.

'MAGUIRE!' he thundered.

The master of the demesne had been reposing in his armchair with a foolish dreamy smile on his face. But now, before he could stop himself, he leaped up and, with a stamping of boots, came rigidly to attention.

'Sir!'

'What the devil have you been up to? What's all this about Juno and people in the Park?'

'Sir!'

'Do you want the whole bloody house burned down?'

'Sir! Permission to speak, sir?'

'Refused.' Phrases welled up that Francis hardly realized he knew. 'You are under arrest!'

'Sir!'

'Don't you dare stir from this room until I give you leave. You are a disgrace to the Army. Brawling, drinking . . . A nice time I had of it with your Flanagan. And now you're off again.'

Maguire made a feeble attempt to arrange his scattered ideas.

'Mr Francis, sir, all I done . . .'

'Less guff. Now mind, here you stay until further orders. Got that?'

'Sir!'

Francis dashed from the room, banging the door. Maguire fell into his chair again and, with tremulous hands, replenished his glass. Well I'll be buggered, he thought dazedly, if you wouldn't swear it was the old man hisself! He had only seen the Major lose his hair a very few times, but they lived in his memory. It soon blew over, but was cruel while it lasted. And here he was, under arrest, just for claiming his rights and keeping things orderly. It wasn't fair, and it wasn't lawful neither, Mr Francis had no powers . . .

Soon the whisky bottle was empty and the horrible part of it was, he dare not go in search of another. He dared not leave his very own room until Mr Francis said he could. That was the Army for you, took all your independence away. Unsteadily, he walked across to the bell and pushed it. Nobody came. That Mrs Jeffars. He pushed again and again with all his might, and still nothing happened. No bloody service. *No discipline.* Showers, the lot. He sat down again, lost in maudlin self-pity, and after a while fell asleep, filling the room with his thunderous snores.

58

# Chapter Eight

Marigold, meanwhile, was above in Spion Kop, waiting for Francis to come and collect her. At last she had finished the packing. They had brought next to nothing with them but, in a familiar fashion, her suitcase seemed to have shrunk of itself in the course of their stay. All she had picked up here was a length of Irish tweed, an Aran Island sweater, the cutest model donkey and cart, a curly ram's horn and a piece of bog oak, weird and lovely in form, rubbed smooth by the centuries of immersion, and yet there had been no end of trouble in getting the case to shut.

Now, somewhat fatigued, she was sitting on it and thinking vaguely of this and that, of how they should get away, of the journey ahead, of Irish life and was it always like this, and above all, of whether she wasn't sorry to leave. Nothing really mattered now except to be with Francis, but still . . . It was all so strange and funny and beautiful. In a day or so the moon would be full again, and if these cloudless skies kept up, the hounds would be baying their hearts out to it, as before. She would never forget that thrilling salutation, the longest day she lived . . .

At this moment Francis came hurrying in, breathless, and announced that they could not go.

'Maguire set Juno on some trippers,' he panted. 'And they pretend that she bit them all. They have asked the Guards to shoot her. I will shoot anyone who attempts it. I have also put Maguire under arrest. Now I must go after these people and buy them off.'

'Quite a programme,' Marigold observed. 'I saw Juno down by the lake as we came in, rummaging in a heap of trash. Let's go and look for blood on the grass before we do anything else.'

'Good idea. Come on!'

There was no blood on the picnic ground, nor any trace of combat whatever. Juno had returned to it after her walk and

59

polished off the remnants of the feast. All that was left was some Irish Fairygold Cheese, which she had spurned, and a few bottles of Guinness, which she had not been able to open. Now, comatose and replete, she was lying contentedly in the sun surrounded by paper bags, plastic cups, hair-curlers, and fragments of the chicken carcase.

'Damned liars!' Francis snapped, glowering at the mess. 'Said they got out of their car for a moment to look at the view, and Juno sprang on them at once.'

'Well, they had to think up a scenario. It would have humiliated them to admit they were just plain scared at the sight of her. See here, Francis, why don't you let me handle this? I'll know how to talk them round.'

'What makes you think that?'

'Why, because it's just like the coloured people at home.'

This anthropological note cause Francis to break into laughter. 'You and those darkies of yours!'

'I'm serious. They'll run a mile from their own shadow and swear it was a ghost coming after them. Same thing here. I'll just play them along and sympathise, and they'll cool off gradually.'

'All right, then.' She would do better than he, with her coaxing and cooing. He would make matters worse, questioning their phantom bites and laughing at their groundless fear. 'I will keep watch over Juno. The man is a Denis Halloran, school teacher, in Ballinaduff. Ask anyone which his house is, they always know. Remember to drive on the left, and watch for cattle and drunks on the road.'

'Shouldn't I ask Maguire before taking the automobile?'

'No. He is under arrest, I tell you.'

'My, my, my, these feudal Irish customs.'

Accompanied by Juno, Francis watched her set out on the mission, his humour fully restored. Fifty minutes to Ballinaduff and back, say half an hour to appease Mr Halloran, leaving ample time before the last train to Dublin. An air taxi to London, if need be, the dawn flight to Paris, breakfast at home on the Quai Voltaire. Coffee, croissants, sanity, civilization . . . He went upstairs and brought the luggage down to the hall in readiness. Next he looked in at the drawing room, intending to

60

patch things up with the humbled Maguire and inform him of the arrangements.

Maguire was still asleep and snoring, his head lolling forward on his chest. Francis shouted at him and finally shook him, but could not rouse him sufficiently for his purpose. Maguire stirred, opened his eyes, and muttered 'Sugar off, mate!' after which he lapsed into slumber again. His previous soldierly conduct must have been a simple reflex action. Laughing, Francis wrote a message to say the car would be left at Ballina station and put it beside the empty decanter: then with a feeling that all was in train and all ends neatly tied, he retired to the library to wait.

He ought to have known better. He should have remembered that well-laid plans, particularly those involving time, are sure to fall apart in Ireland. Why this is so, has never been explained. Some thinkers believe that the country holds a spirit, or Djinn, whom the very idea of an ordered schedule will goad to fury. But, whatever the reason for it may be, the fact is clear and unmistakeable.

Even when the Rector's mild voice was raised in the hall, asking if anyone were home, Francis remained unconscious of a threat. He was actually pleased by the sound of it: there was time and to spare, and he had not altogether relished the thought of leaving without a single goodbye. Hastening to open the library door he welcomed the visitor, brought him in, offered tea and remarked on the beautiful weather. The Rector concurred as to this, but refused all refreshment and took a chair with a look on his face that suggested an unquiet mind.

'My dear Francis,' he began, 'please do not misunderstand or resent what I am going to say. Naturally, you will have wished to be left to yourself at the present time. But you have now been here almost a month, and it is a disappointment to me, and to all of us, that so far we have not seen you in church.'

Shades of the prison house! thought Francis: well for him, that he was soon to be gone. 'I am sorry to hear that, Rector,' he said. 'Frankly, I am not a church-goer, nor is my wife.'

Dr Thornton looked more distressed than ever, indeed, quite woebegone. 'I know, my dear boy, young people are apt to fall away now,' he sighed. 'But in your position! Your father always read the Lessons, as did his own father before him when at home. We have all assumed that you would do likewise.'

'I, Rector? At my age?' Francis was really surprised. 'What would the parishioners have to say? Surely, Beaulieu, or Fishy . . .'

'Colonel Beaulieu has kindly helped us out these past few Sundays,' the Rector replied. 'But he does not care for it much. And his habit of thinking aloud is unfortunate. I distinctly heard him mutter that the Gospel for the day was a lot of old tripe last week, as he was going down from the lectern. And as for Fi . . . ah, Lord Carageen, he is somewhat . . . not altogether . . . that is, there is good in us all and only God can know our hearts, but nevertheless. . . Anyhow, Francis, you as the owner of Castle Reef are the right person to take this on. You are the first man now of our little community.'

'I had never thought of myself in that way,' said Francis. 'Or I should naturally have let you know that we are returning to Paris.'

'To Paris! But my dear boy . . .' The Rector was dumbfounded. 'What can have induced you to take such a step? When do you mean to go? And for how long?'

'Immediately. This afternoon. As for my future plans, if you will forgive me, I would rather not discuss them. You will understand presently.'

There was a silence, the Rector staring unhappily at the floor. 'I have no wish to pry into your affairs,' he said at length. 'And no right either. It was shock that led me to put the questions I did. Well, I must not detain you, if you are to travel so soon.' He started to rise, but sank down again. 'There was another point I wanted to raise, a minor one, but still of importance to us. The harvest festival is approaching. Your dear father was always most liberal, with flowers, fruit, vegetables, that kind of thing. It goes to the hospital afterwards. Bless me, the mammoth pumpkin he gave us last year! Matron told me, they needed a saw to cut it. May we hope to receive the Castle's bounty as usual?'

Trapped, cornered, with nothing left but to speak the truth!

'It doesn't depend on me, Rector,' Francis said uncomfortably. 'It isn't mine to give.' He paused, then blurted out: 'My father has left the place to Maguire.'

'Maguire!' cried the Rector, aghast. 'My dear boy, can you be serious?'

'Entirely so,' Francis assured him, adopting as light a tone as he could. 'Why not? I am sure he will make a very good landlord.'

'No doubt, no doubt, Maguire is an excellent fellow, most worthy, and we are all as one in the eyes of God. But not, I fear,' sighed the Rector, 'in those of the parish. There will be a rumpus, if not a furore. What an astonishing thing for your father to do! Did you realize what was to happen?'

'Not until Goodchild informed me, when at last he came down. I was wondering why I did not hear from him – it seems, he shrank from breaking the news.'

'I am not surprised,' the Rector groaned. 'I hardly know myself if I am on my head or on my heels.'

Francis was moved to pity by the old man's distress, so much greater than his own. 'I shall write to Maguire about the festival,' he promised. 'At the moment, he is unwell. I'm sure he will give you whatever my father gave. And who knows,' he went on gaily, 'perhaps he will read the Lessons for you!'

The Rector's woebegone face relaxed a little at this. 'Oh my dear boy,' he chuckled, 'you always could see the comical side of things.' But his amusement was shortlived. 'Ah well, I must leave you. Please give my kindest regards to dear Maria. Who knows when we shall meet again?' If ever, he thought drearily. 'This has been strange and heavy news, Francis. Goodbye, and God bless you.'

He was out of the house and on his way before it occurred to the dear boy that nothing had been said as to the news being confidential. But no matter: Marigold would be back any minute now and, as far as the two of them were concerned, the curtain rung down. The little rule of Irish life referred to above, he had still not recollected.

Shattered, the Rector toiled along the river bank and on coming to the bridge leaned against it, to collect his powers before passing Miss Hackle's cottage. Then a car pulled up and there was Dr McLeod, asking if something were wrong and if he would like a lift home. The offer was gladly accepted, and rewarded by the juiciest piece of information ever to come in the doctor's way. Having dropped the Rector, he hurried home to pass it on to his wife: and she, when the pair of them had chewed it over sufficiently, telephoned to Mrs Beaulieu.

Whether or not, as some believed, there was a magic in the local telephone wires, causing items of interest which travelled down them to volatilize and waft through the air, in no time at all Ballinaween was talking of nothing else.

Most of the people did little more than gasp, cluck and exclaim: it was too early to analyse, probe and take up positions, for a thrill of this magnitude was enough in itself. But a certain number shook in their shoes, namely, those stalwart regulars of the pub who had set on Maguire the night before. Denis, Matty, Joe, Peadar and Liam all were employed by the Castle, with good wages, free milk, potatoes, firewood and housing. The big-mouthed boyo they had chastized for pulling their legs in fact had spoken the truth and now was their master – or, would it be more accurate to say, might have been?

When the blow fell they were together in the pub once more, having taken a day off to nurse their wounds. Maguire had defended himself with vigour, dealing out bruises, bumps on the head, aching shins and wobbly teeth with a will. They were in high feather, none the less, happily debating how much they dared sting Mr Francis for. He had met Flanagan's claim in full, like the decent boy he was, and surely to God he would do no less by them? But even as they conferred, casting about in their minds for a reasonably exorbitant figure, a man from the village flew in with the hideous revelation.

It was some little while before it really sank in. Their first reaction was a sense of utter betrayal. They had often argued, in their cups, that it was wrong for one old family to keep so much in its fist and that justice required the People to take it away. But now it had passed to the people, in the shape of Maguire, and the prospect appalled them. Everyone knew, whatever radical views he might spout, that the Quality were the best employers, being apparently blind, deaf and half-witted. A man like Maguire was up to their little tricks, and would drive them worse than the African slaves of yore. Nevertheless, it was clear that somehow or other he would have to be placated, and also, that there was no time to lose.

They decided to go up to the Castle now and see him, express the hope that their innocent fun had been taken as such, assure him of their continuing warm regard. It was after all the unwritten law of Irish pubs that whatever took place of an evening was cancelled out by the following day: were it not so, the social life of the country would come to an end. Of his elevation, they would of course know nothing: it was to be a simple friendly call.

The plan met with entire approval. Having swallowed a few more jars in quick succession, the five of them squeezed into Matty's ancient Morris Minor. But halfway up the Castle drive another idea struck the leader and he called on Matty to stop while they discussed it. At which of the Castle doors should they present themselves? Properly, it should be at the front, since Maguire was now the master; but they were not supposed to be aware of that. Yet, if they went to the back, as if he were still a servant, he might take offence. If they knocked at the office where they went to collect their pay, most likely no one would hear them; and if at any of the other entrances, the conservatory for example, it might be seen as a liberty.

They argued the problem up and down for more than half an hour. It is curious how, in Ireland, matters of no importance whatever will keep minds working at full stretch almost indefinitely, while complicated issues are dealt with by a few blows of a stick or a burst of high explosive. At last, however, their choice fell on the one proposed to begin with, namely, the front.

When he heard the knock, Francis was pacing fretfully to and fro, wondering when Marigold would appear. There was still time to catch the train, but she had by a long way exceeded that allowed for her expedition. He should not have agreed to her going like that, in a strange car, through strange country. It would be in keeping with things if she, gamely driving on the unaccustomed left, ran slap into a drunk, advancing bemusedly on the right. He now ran to the door, hoping for news of her, to find himself confronted with five sheepish countrymen, flushed with drink and generally looking the worse for wear.

65

'What the blazes do you want?' he barked, to a rumble of sympathy from Juno.

'We were looking for Mr Maguire, Mr Francis, sir,' said Denis apprehensively.

'Were you, indeed! Was it you who knocked him about? Well, you shan't see him.' And Francis made to shut the door.

'But Mr Francis, there's urgent business in it!'

'Never mind.'

The door was closing. Another moment and it would be too late. Instinctively, Denis leaned his shoulder on it and vigorously pushed it wide again. He meant no harm in the world, merely wished to continue pleading with Mr Francis, but Juno did not realize that. Like many wellbred dogs, she had an acute sense of protocol, and she was already displeased that such obviously backdoor people had ventured to knock at the front. This new liberty exhausted her patience altogether: bounding forward, deaf to their cries, she herded them angrily down the steps and into the car, just as she had done with the trespassers, gently nipping their ankles where she could and growling defiance at them once they were safe inside.

Francis was too taken up with his thoughts to notice that history was repeating itself or to worry about possible repercussions. 'Good girl,' he said briefly. 'Come on back, now.'

And they returned to the library, Juno to stretch out on the hearthrug, Francis to continue nervously pacing here and there, wondering what the devil was going on.

# Chapter Nine

Marigold had not been delayed by collision with drunken drivers or animals running loose on the road, or by any other usual event; and she had easily found the Halloran dwelling, pacifying the inmates in no time at all. They had, however, insisted on her remaining to tea, which she took to mean a cup of tea and a sandwich or biscuit. When it arrived, after an interval, it proved to be an orgy of bacon and eggs, potato cakes swimming in butter, brack, and peaches with cream, washed down by strong black tea, followed by stout and the offer of poteen. That, indeed, had held her up, especially as the Hallorans would not hear of her skipping a single item. Even so, she would have got back to the Castle with an hour to spare, had it not been for an occurrence on the way.

Somewhere along the Ballinaduff-Ballinaween road, which runs over a stretch of bog with a steep bank down on either side, she was waved to by an elderly man. She remembered seeing him at the funeral party, a Lord someone, she rather thought, in any case a friend of the family and apparently in need of a lift. She therefore pulled up and the man quickly got in, looking at her in a somewhat peculiar fashion; and his reply to her question, where did he want to go, was more peculiar still.

'Nowhere, m'dear,' he said. 'Just wanted to get to know you. No chance of a quiet chat in that crush, was there? I'm Carrageen, but you must call me Fishy. Old friend of Arthur's, y'know. Sandhurst, that kind of thing. The Barracloughs certainly know how to pick 'em,' he continued, ogling her with a watery eye. 'What do you say, we run out to my place and have a snifter?'

Lord Carrageen was at once the terror and the joke of the county. In his younger days he had made advances, with much success, to every attractive woman or girl he met. He was uncommonly handsome then, tall and slim with a mane of

67

curly hair and laughing green eyes. Now he stooped, was fat and baldish, with crimson bloated features and a filmy stare. But inwardly there had been no change at all, and he continued to burn with the ardour of twenty-five. For the life of him, he never could see why his looks should make any difference. Undeterred by failure and rebuff, he followed his inclinations, convinced that if only the women would try him out they would feel themselves rewarded.

Unaware of all this, Marigold was placidly driving on. 'I'm afraid I have to get back,' she said. 'But I will take you home with pleasure if you tell me where it is.'

'I'm your next door neighbour,' his lordship replied. In fact, his ancestral hall was a good twenty miles from the Castle, but the humbler buildings between did not, as far as he was concerned, exist. 'Rotten old barn on the hill. You'll have to come in for a moment or two. I'll show you my collection of snuff-boxes.'

'I can't, Francis and I are catching the Dublin train,' Marigold said.

'Going off already!' he cried in dismay. 'Damn it, you've only just come. Be a sport, train isn't till six, you've whips of time.'

'Francis is expecting me, I'm sorry.' Really, as if she hadn't enough to do, remembering where things on the dashboard were and to keep on the left of the road!

'Well, give me a kiss, then,' he entreated. 'Just one!'

'Hey, there, ease off! I'm an old married woman.'

'What of it? Who's to know? Why throw your luck away?'

With that, he ran his arm round her waist and planted a vigorous kiss on her ear. Taken by surprise she swerved violently and the Mercedes left the road, rammed a tree and turned over twice before coming to rest on the bog below. One of the headlamps came bowling after, taking its time as if there were not much point in trying to catch the motor up. The windscreen was shattered, and the gleaming bonnet all buckled.

'Well, at least we are not on fire,' Marigold observed. She had switched the engine off directly they hit the tree, and now was brushing particles of the windscreen from her dress and hair.

'Sorry about that,' said her passenger gruffly. 'Good thing you kept your head. But how was I to know...don't tell me you've never been kissed before!'

Marigold tried to start the engine, but there was no response. 'Here we stay, I guess,' she drawled.

'I'll have to go and get help.' He sounded faintly aggrieved. 'Damn it, this door won't open.'

Marigold tried hers. 'Nor does this. Maybe one of the others will.'

She was about to climb over the back rest when the squad car drew up and three Guards came scrambling down the bank in a hurry, the Sergeant among them. While the two underlings set the prisoners free, he pensively took note of the damage, his lips pursed in a soundless whistle.

'A write-off! I'm afraid you won't get twopence, Mrs,' he said, with lugubrious satisfaction. 'We were following you. There was no need for that accident, none at all. Evening, my lord.'

'Evening, Sergeant. My silly fault. I distracted the lady's attention.' Lord Carrageen felt he must do the honourable thing, but embarrassment showed in the deeper crimson of his face and the way his voice came out, as if he were gargling.

'That won't make any odds, my lord, not with the insurance. Could you find your own way now, I wonder? We've only one seat going. We were bound for the Castle as it was. There's more complaints about the dog.'

'Certainly, of course. I was out walking when Mrs Barra-clough kindly gave me a lift.'

The Sergeant was plunged in thought as the car drove on and only spoke when it turned into the Castle avenue. 'I can't make this out at all, ma'am,' he said in a peevish tone. 'It wouldn't be how your man was a bit too friendly, like?'

'No, I was dodging a rabbit. And I never drove a right-hand wheeler before, nor on the left. And the road itself was kind of bouncy.'

'That's the bog underneath it, ma'am. You should drive down the middle, like everyone else.'

Marigold had often wondered at this regional custom, and was much amused by his explanation of it. Francis, on the other hand, was not in the least amused by anything the law had to say, whether concerning the accident, the fate of the car or the purpose of the Sergeant's errand.

'I suppose they told you, Juno tore them to shreds,' he said severely. 'There were five of them, all plastered, and they refused to leave. Denis Mangan actually tried to push his way through the door. Of course she wouldn't have that.'

The Sergeant heaved a sigh. The men had drink taken, no doubt of it, but he dared not say so without a police doctor had examined them and confirmed it. There had been actions, successful ones, over that kind of indiscretion. 'You'll have to put a muzzle on him, Mr Francis, or tie him in. Two complaints in one day!'

'I shall do neither. Muzzle, indeed! I haven't got such a thing.'

'You could maybe get a bit of a strap and fasten it round his mout'.'

'So I could. And I could tie one of her front paws under her chin, or a bloody great stone to her collar,' said Francis, referring to other local practices. 'But, you see, I won't. None of the parties involved had any business here.'

'He's a dangerous animal, all the same, and he'll have to be kept in control up here as much as anywhere else.'

Now they were joined by the culprit herself, who stood in the doorway eyeing the visitor with extreme disapprobation. She saw at once that here was another backdoor person trying to force a way in by the front. An intelligent dog, she nevertheless lacked the power of abstract thought, the grasp of concepts such as the State and the privileges of lowborn people in State employ: Guards and postmen alike, in her opinion, belonged to an intolerably bumptious class, their very uniform a studied insult. Slowly her lips receded, baring her splendid teeth.

The Sergeant did not wait to argue, but hurried down the steps and hopped nimbly into the car. 'Don't let me have to speak again, Mr Francis,' he implored through the window. 'I have me duty to do. There's no law in this land,' he commented bitterly, as the car moved away. 'We might be in darkest Africa. And gentry is the worst of the lot.'

Her husband's reaction to the other events of that afternoon

70

was the very reverse of what Marigold had expected. Thinking the truth might cause unpleasantness, she repeated her fib about the rabbit, whereupon he went into fits of laughter. 'Come off it,' he chuckled. 'The old ram made a pass at you. Did he promise to show you his snuff-boxes?'

'Why, yes. Do you mean to say you're not annoyed?'

'Devil a bit. We all know Fishy. And you needn't put on dog, what is more. He does that to every woman under the age of ninety who isn't an out-and-out scarecrow.' He went on to regale her with anecdotes of his lordship's career, how he would boast of triumphs never enjoyed, disappearing from time to time and letting everyone know he was off on an escapade. 'He once put it round that he was taking an actress to Monte Carlo,' he said, with tears of merriment in his eyes. 'And the Beaulieus ran across him in a London tea-shop, all alone and fuming about the service.'

On the other hand, when she told him how kind and amenable the Hallorans were, and how they had entertained her, he was extremely vexed. 'I like their infernal cheek,' he exclaimed. 'That kind of person never knows where to stop. Stuffing you with their beastly food! And they always have a motive for what they do. They'll be dropping your name all over the town, and probably expect you to ask them here.'

This prophecy, however, recalled them both to the present. Their plans had broken down, there could be no question of leaving until the affair of the car was settled. And there was Juno's safety to be considered, Francis said; these brutes were capable of putting down poisoned meat. You could buy strychnine by the barrel in these parts and no one raised an eyebrow, but let anyone ask for a pound of yeast and he was a marked man, suspected of keeping a still. No, here they must stay until this particular bit of nonsense blew over.

'If Maguire will allow it,' Marigold said, with a mischievous smile.

'I should like to see him do anything else!' retorted the rightful heir.

But that night he had a dream of a kind which before the move to Paris had troubled him frequently. It was not a recurring nightmare, for the circumstances were always different, but the crux of it and the fear it inspired were the same. He would be sinking into a bog, or taking hold of something which stuck to him fast, or beating the walls of a room without any egress. Now he dreamed of a giant octopus which tried to enfold him and which, after he had frantically swum ashore, came marching grimly towards him over the sand. He woke to find Marigold gently shaking his arm and asking what went on, he was whimpering like a puppy.

# Chapter Ten

Very soon the village and surrounding hamlets, indeed, the county itself and beyond, had recovered from the shock of the news concerning the Major's will. Now many were hard at work exercising their Irish gift for putting flesh on the bones of a story. What had induced the Major to take this step? He had always doted on the boy. It could not have been his choice of a wife, for the poor man had never seen her, never come round after the stroke occasioned by the news of his engagement. The Will must have been drawn up already. You would have to go further back to find the truth. The boy's refusal to join the Army must have been a terrible disappointment, for all the Major said nothing about it. Undoubtedly, the key to the riddle lay somewhere in that refusal, and the only question was, where?

The more people put their minds to this, the clearer the answer they found. The thought which had fleetingly struck the Major himself, and been dismissed by Maguire out of hand, soon gained acceptance. In these days of republican terror, Francis had feared for his safety: he was a coward, and the Major could not forgive it, were he twenty times his son. Added proof of the theory's correctness lay in the choice of Maguire to supplant him, Maguire the intrepid, who had rushed through that hail of bullets to save his superior's life. Now they came to think of it, they had noted the yellow streak in Francis themselves. Why else should a man refuse to hunt, what other reason could he have? Why else should he keep a fierce dog to guard him? The evidence piled up. Then he was an intellectual and a bookworm and, while few of his critics had met such people before, they all knew what they were like.

Other and stranger rumours were flying around, begun and spread by Quirke the solicitor. Why had so long elapsed before the contents of the Will were known? It must be, that Francis had found a copy at home and, assuming it was the only one, destroyed it. Mr Goodchild had hastened down from Dublin to warn him of the peril in which he stood and frighten him with the law. But Mr Goodchild had left again early next morning, so that whatever he had to say in the matter must have been said on the previous day. Yet – mark this well – at a dinner that same evening, with Mr Quirke present, Maguire had performed the duties of a butler, obviously unaware of his real position. Francis had persisted in trying to hush it up, perhaps had bribed the lawyer to hold his tongue. Purely by chance, Maguire had overheard him boasting to Marigold of his crime after the guests had gone. Then, rather than face exposure, the villain decided to flee to France and would have been there now, but for the mishap to Maguire's car, purloined for the escape.

It was perhaps less a matter of putting flesh on bones than of weaving a tapestry, taking this strand of wool, discarding that, to fit in with the pattern. Among the discarded were Colonel Beaulieu's dogged assertion that it was Arthur Barraclough DSO who had saved Maguire and not the other way round; the Rector's mild remonstrance about the hunting, which Francis had often told him he could not abide; the fact of Juno's acquisition at nine week's old by the Major himself, while Francis was away, and the presence of Lord Carrageen, not Francis, in the allegedly stolen car. And once the tapestry was complete, the woollen strands composing it miraculously turned to wire, never to be dissolved short of soaking in acid. Now that Francis had nothing to offer, kindly local feeling towards him died away. The people grieved for the father, condemned the wrong to Maguire and were fully persuaded that Francis was as bad an egg as any to be found in Victorian melodrama.

Had they but known it, in the days that followed they had much to thank the young man for. Maguire had no objection whatever to his remaining as long as he wished, indeed, he jumped at the idea with frank relief. Mrs Jeffars had kept her word and departed, and Maguire now himself proposed to stay in his old quarters while the young couple were there and to let the Castle arrangements continue much as they always had. In this he was prompted by more than simple goodness, for he

74

felt that he was moving in strange dark places, badly in need of guidance and support.

At the same time, certain views that he held, long suppressed, now came bubbling to the surface.

'I daresay!' he said, when the matter of the harvest festival was laid before him. 'Bloody scroungers! Always looking for something or other. The Major was far too good. It's going to be different now, I can tell you.'

But Francis expounded the doctrine of *noblesse oblige* to such effect that a liberal supply of flowers, fruit and vegetables went off to St Andrews as usual. The promise of central heating for the church was ratified too, and neighbours would still be welcome to shoot and fish. When it came to the kennelling of the hounds, however, Maguire showed fight. As if their yowling and yelping were not enough, the smelly carcases on which they fed were costing a packet. Expressed in terms of Scotch – Maguire taking a bottle thereof as the currency unit – a week's food for the pack was roughly equivalent to a month's hard drinking. When the stables were put at the Hunt's disposal, nothing had been said as to the animals' keep. Somehow or other it had drifted on to the Castle books and Maguire was not going to wear it. Even here Francis finally carried the day, with the double plea of what his father would wish and his wife's distress were the pack to be removed. She had taken a fancy to the creatures, knew many of them by name and regarded them altogether as part of the household. Maguire yielded; and the Hunt, which had been on tenterhooks while it supposed the decision to lie with Francis, breathed again, thanking its stars for a sound champ at the helm after all.

These were matters that largely concerned the upper crust. Maguire also had views on the manner in which the estate was run and the deportment of those who worked there. They would turn up at any old hour, or not at all, and if needed for some special purpose were usually found enjoying a smoke or a cup of tea. When they knocked off, whatever implement they had been using, spade, scythe, loy, hammer, was flung to the ground and left in the rain. The cows would bellow for someone to milk them while their keepers pondered the racing results or chuckled over a piece of gossip. When a tractor broke down,

75

it was left to itself, as if in time it would recover without assistance.

But what exasperated Maguire beyond words was, that no one was ever to blame. In the Army, a prudent man of course took steps to ensure that, if something went wrong, he was 'covered'. Here there was no need for it, because there was no connection between what happened and any human act whatsoever. Hayricks went on fire, not through a cigarette stub being thrown on them, but because the Almighty wished it. A tar barrel would explode and devastate all around, not because someone forgot to take the lid off at heating, but for private reasons of its own. Sheep wandered off and poisoned themselves with bane because such was the habit of sheep, and a broken fence or a gap in the hedge had nothing to do with it.

All these things, and others, Maguire had noted with helpless indignation from afar, and now he decided on reform. His plan, simple, clear and grand as are the plans of genius, or lunacy, was to treat the staff as an Army unit. The men should parade every morning to receive their orders, and again at the end of the day, when Maguire had completed his inspection. Defaulters would be placed on a charge, with stoppage of pay or extra duty as the consequence, while the deserving would get promotion. Men were to sign for any equipment issued and be held responsible for it. Of teabreaks there should be only two, mid-morning and mid-afternoon; and the signal for these, as for the start and close of the dinner hour, was to be a bugle call, blown by himself.

'I'll shake 'em,' he declared. 'Shake 'em to the toenails, I will.'

Francis was sorely tempted to approve a scheme so rich in probable entertainment, but wiser thoughts prevailed.

'I don't think you should do that, Maguire,' he said. 'The men would never stand it. And if they walked out, you would only get others exactly like them, or none at all.'

'It's what I always done, inside, more or less,' Maguire retorted. 'I never stood no nonsense, no, not from the ESB itself. Haven't you noticed how everything here is in working order and good repair? The Rector's waiting a year and more to get

76

the roof of his greenhouse mended. It doesn't do to be soft with the likes of them round here.'

The alacrity with which carpenters, plumbers, electricians, answered a call from the Castle had not, in fact, been due to Maguire's bluff soldierly ways but because the Major settled accounts at once, however preposterous, and always took an interest in the workmen and their families.

Francis allowed this to pass, and went on. 'And then, there's McKenna, aren't you forgetting him?' McKenna was the estate agent or factor, an Ulster Protestant who had been there for many years. Once he too had indulged in dreams like those of Maguire, but long bitter experience had taught him. 'He's in charge, after all. Surely you won't go over his head?'

'Maybe he needs a shake-up as well.'

'Hang it, the place doesn't do badly. It brings in a decent revenue, better than anywhere else round here.'

'I reckon it could be doubled,' said Maguire, with a gleam of avarice in his eye. 'Buncher lazy good-for-nothing so-and-so's. But you're soft, Mr Francis, pardon the liberty, soft as the Major hisself.'

'Yes. He was pretty soft with us too, wasn't he?'

Maguire was about to reply when he suddenly thought better of it, and looked sheepish. Profiting by this rare occurrence, Francis went on to develop the theme of *noblesse oblige* and its drawbacks. People of standing must expect to be plundered and diddled by those they employed – at this, Maguire actually hung his head – and not always look for their own, like sharp little tradesmen. Of course they were well aware of what happened but they turned a blind eye, like the Russian nobility of Tsarist times, supposedly so tyrannical, in fact, as could be learned from novels and memoirs of the day, a pattern of easygoing forbearance . . .

'And much good it did 'em,' muttered Maguire.

Nothing further was said of a shake-up, however, and the old happy confusion of life carried on. Reassured and contented, everyone gave Maguire the credit for this as well; and the men involved in the fracas at Flanagan's, hearing no more of it, thought him the finest sportsman out.

Francis himself was agreeably surprised when the question

of the Mercedes came up. About that he had many qualms, for it never was easy to prise insurance from Irish companies, even in a watertight case. So often and so flagrantly were they swindled, they lived in a state of chronic suspicion. Here, the car was legally in a limbo, the registered owner dead, the new one's possession as yet unproved; the accident had taken place on a clear road, and Mrs Barraclough's licence did not allow her to drive in Ireland. No lawyer, not even Quirke, could have slid over facts like these. There was nothing to hope for, and nothing to be done but order a replacement, a most confounded expense.

When he put this to Maguire, that independent thinker again had views of his own. He did not want a Mercedes. It always beat him, he said, that the Major, having gone to the trouble of licking the Jerries, should then buy a blooming old Jerry car. He wanted something smaller and British. Francis pointed out that the roads were rough and British cars had a way of falling to pieces; but Maguire merely sniffed, as much as to say that British cars were entitled to please themselves. A Marina, now, or a Hillman, nothing fancy nor with a ruinous consumption of petrol, that was the long and the short of it, and Mr Francis would oblige him by meeting his wishes.

After some argument for decency's sake, Francis thankfully gave in. A Marina was ordered and delivered, providing a fresh instalment in the saga of his misdeeds. Not content with grabbing Maguire's car for his getaway, and wrecking it, he had fobbed him off with a cheap little runabout in its place, as befitting his lowly origins. The good old Major must be turning in his grave, while your man walked about, bold as brass, without a feather off him. Occupying the best rooms still, it was rumoured, while Maguire was pent in his small parlour beside the kitchen and his smaller bedroom above it. The arrogant young fellow had refused to accept the position, and the Major's loyal servant – and preserver – acquiesced in that refusal, too humble to claim his right, content in the place allotted him.

# Chapter Eleven

How wide of the mark the local interpretation was, and how deeply Maguire had pondered the words of his mentor, made itself known some three weeks afterwards. The period intervening was a busy one for Francis, what with the purchase of the new car, the raising and disposal of the old – to the general surprise, as the bog was strewn with similar corpses which had been there for years – and various legal matters of his own. Everything had taken longer than it would have anywhere else, but now it all was settled. There had been no further demand for the destruction, tying or muzzling of Juno; and Francis was turning his thoughts to Paris again.

Then one morning came a telephone call from Colonel Beaulieu, speaking in his capacity of Master of Foxhounds.

'Er . . . that you, Francis?' He cleared his throat, in an embarrassed kind of way. 'Er . . . cubbing's over. First hunt of the season on Tuesday. Do I take it, we meet at your . . . at the Castle this year?'

'I imagine you do,' Francis replied. 'Maguire doesn't intend to make any changes, I know. Shall I check with him?'

'Please. Can you do it today? Barrie wants to send the notices out. He has only just raised the point. No use asking if you'll come with us?'

'None at all.'

'Lazy young blighter.' With a chuckle, the Colonel rang off. A few of the legends collecting round Francis had come to his ears, going in at one and straight out of the other; but nobody had been rash enough to pass on the theory that he was a coward.

Francis set off on his errand at once, hoping to find Maguire in. He knew old Beaulieu would be on tenterhooks until this all-important query was answered, and private business was often taking the lord of the manor to Ballinaduff these days. There was no sign of him now in his lair, nor in the vast sepulchral kitchen, where Marigold was hard at work on one of her flower arrangements. She was continually unearthing frightfulness he never even knew the house contained: among it, huge and hideous Victorian vases in the form of a boat, a swan or a Grecian urn, which she would fill with elaborate bouquets to give, she said, a homey touch to rooms decorated chiefly with swords, medals, flags and paintings of military exploits.

'Isn't this cute?' she said, surveying a tangle of yellow leaves, scarlet berries and silvery Old Man's Beard with satisfaction. 'Guess what it's meant to be.' For all her compositions stood for something or other.

'Preparing the Bonfire?' he suggested. 'Or, Miss Hackle's Hallowe'en Hat?'

'No, you dope. The Spirit of Autumn.'

'To be sure, so it is. Silly of me. Where's old Maguire? The Hunt is fussing about its Meet.'

'I'm not surprised,' she said absently, poking another spray into the thicket. 'There's a load of it out in the yard right now, smelling just fierce. I'll say this for hounds, they're not picky eaters.'

'The MEET, darling. The hunting season is on us, and the first Meet was always here. They want to know if Maguire will let them come. He probably will, but I have to make sure.'

'He went up to his room a while ago with a great big box in his arms,' said Marigold. 'Hugging it, like it was precious. I didn't hear him come down.'

Francis went to the foot of the stairway leading up to Maguire's room and called out to know if that landed gentleman was there. The answer that came was curiously shrill and flustered, rather as if Maguire were a lady who had 'disappeared' behind a bush, and was in no fit state to be seen.

'Just a minute, sir. Don't come up.'

'I only want to ask if the Hunt can meet here? Next Tuesday? The Colonel was on just now.'

'Course he can, and welcome. I've been lookin' forward to it. But, Mr Francis, I shan't be available to pass the drinks about.'

The custom was to fortify the hunters with stirrup-cups of cherry brandy and sloe gin before they rode away.

'Naturally not. No one expects you to. My wife and I will see to that.' And Francis retired, to put the Master's mind at ease.

Punctually at half-past ten on the following Tuesday morning the Hunt began to arrive, and a brave stirring sight they were. One and all, they were inclined to be shabby in their everyday clothes, indifferent to frayed cuffs and elbows, shapeless hats and baggy knees, even to rents, holes or patches. For the Meet, however, they turned out spick and span as the Household Brigade, the men with their pink jackets and white breeches spotless, all with their stocks snowy and neatly tied, their boots polished until they shone, and their horses' grooming and tack to match. As far as they were concerned, it was clear, this was the true, serious, business of life. The horses impatiently threw up their heads, whinnied, pawed the earth, and danced about, urging their riders to look sharp and be off.

For all that, a certain tension could be felt in the air this morning. Tighe the huntsman and Bob the Whip were a saturnine pair at any time, but the look on their faces as they rode away to fetch the hounds was unusually sour. Francis, carrying his tray of drinks, had to speak twice before he caught the Colonel's ear.

'I said, will you have sloe gin or cherry brandy, Master?'

'Eh, what's that? Sloe gin, thank you, Francis, very kind, I'm sure. Butler today are you? Good lad.'

'I endeavour to give satisfaction, sir. But is anything wrong?'

The Colonel had absently taken the glass and was staring down the avenue with it in his hand, untasted.

'Eh? No, not really. Four bloody foreigners coming today, and there's still no sign of 'em.'

Foreigners, in his vocabulary, did not as a rule mean persons of different nationality but members of other Hunts who happened to be in the neighbourhood and wanted a run.

'Well, if they don't show up soon, we'll send them after you. Rougemain, I think you said.'

'Yes, but this lot would never find it.' The Colonel swallowed the gin and gave back the glass.

Francis proceeded on his rounds, looking after the men, while Marigold saw to the ladies. The people here assembled were of that Anglo-Irish class that abhorred a plain Mr: if you could not boast a title, like Carrageen or FitzMarlow, you were expected at least to be Colonel, Major, Commander or The, like The O'Barrnock of Barnnock. Men had been driven to enter the Church to avoid the dire appellation, and some of the military ranks, relating to short term service, hardly bore too close an inquiry. As Mr Barraclough, a non-hunting man and not even the Castle's new owner, Francis was made to feel his position: the men were civil enough, but cool and casual; but by the more demonstrative ladies a few barbed little comments were made, which Marigold was at a loss to understand.

Except, that is, for one from Miss Hilary Baggot, whom the Major once had picked as a possible daughter-in-law, and among whose gifts was a notable clarity of expression.

'You really should make Francis hunt, you know,' she said in her booming voice. 'Looks so odd.'

Marigold thought, the Hunt itself looked as odd as anything she had ever clapped eyes on, but she kept this view to herself. 'He doesn't care about it,' she replied, with her usual sweetness of manner. 'And no one can make him do things if he doesn't want to.'

'Safety First!' said Miss Baggot, with a ringing laugh. 'Is that it?'

'Do you mean to suggest, he's afraid?' asked Marigold, her colour rising a little. 'I never knew him scary of anything yet.'

'Well, there must be some reason,' Miss Baggot rejoined. 'And I'm blowed if I can think of another.'

Here she spoke the absolute truth, her range of surmise being uncommonly restricted: but Marigold was deeply hurt and found nothing to say.

Now a clatter of hooves and a joyous yelping announced the return of Tighe and Bob with the pack and, in another moment, they swept round the corner into sight. There were, however, three men with the hounds, instead of two, the third being Maguire, resplendent in hunting kit which, run up by local talent and wrong in every particular, had a distinctly carnival air. He was plainly unconscious of anything amiss, and trotted on ahead of the others to greet the Hunt with expansive warmth.

'Morning, all!' he cried, cheerily. 'Smashin' day! Get yer little drop, did yer? Then a-huntin' we will go!'

To a man and a woman, the Hunt gazed at him in consternation. While they knew how matters stood and realized that he was their host today, they were still unable to think of him except as the noiseless efficient chap who had waited on them so often and for so long. They felt like the eighteenth century Beau, who graciously accepted a wealthy snob's invitation to dinner, only to find with disgust that the fellow expected to sit at the table. And to think that a man 'in this day and age' could be so ignorant as not to know that one had to join a Hunt, be proposed and accepted and pay a subscription, before he could ride! It made you wonder what children learned in all these subsidized schools. Was he cocking a snook at them? There was his get-up . . . From somewhere, somehow, he had procured a stovepipe hat, as worn by Irish priests in days gone by, which added considerably to the clownish effect of the whole.

All were aghast, but none more so than Juno. She had been sitting on the grass, eyeing the Quality with complacent approval. Now she saw Maguire, her own dear Maguire, who fed her, walked her, fondled her, so far forgetting his place as to mingle with it. She pricked her ears and, lifting her front paws rapidly one after the other, as if marking time, softly whined in reproach and concern.

Unaware of the sensation he had caused, Maguire rode up to the Master to do the honours in style; but before he could open his mouth, something occurred to upstage him completely. The four foreigners for whom the Hunt was fretfully waiting arrived, and soon every eye was fixed on them in horror. Here were no spruce experienced riders from neighbouring country, but a motley crew in outlandish clothes who seemingly had never mounted a horse before. In these pinched and straitened times, the MFH had to consent to measures that in his younger days he would have found inconceivable, among them, an arrangement with the Tourist Board. That enterprising body ran a sporting package tour, providing a day of hunting here, of fishing there, of shooting somewhere else, and patronized mainly by Americans who wanted to prattle about it when they got home.

On they came in Indian file, with their bizarre caps, colourful jackets or personalized T-shirts, a camera slung round each neck. There was this of comfort in it, that none of them was likely to stay the course. Although their mounts were at a walk, the rear sportsman already hung on by the mane; and the three in front held their reins at chin-level, while their heels wavered backward and upward in a manner that boded no good. The leader was attempting a jaunty smile, but producing only a sickly grin.

'What's all this, then?' demanded Maguire. The Master was unable to speak.

Juno felt that the world was indeed upside down and that, unless she took charge, there was no telling what might happen next. She flew at the cavalcade with the idea of escorting it back whence it came. But the hacks, their nerves already frayed by amateur handling, lost their heads and panicked. The front two reared and their riders slid to the ground, the third bucked his man off by kicking his heels up behind, and the fourth galloped across to the lake, where she flung herself down and started to roll, deaf to the cries of her cargo.

'I know that mare,' said the MFH, recovering his speech and looking slightly more cheerful. 'From Toddy's in Ballinaduff. Can't resist a wallow. Nearly drowned a fella once.'

Her recent incumbent, still shouting, struggled ashore. The others lay where they fell, gingerly prodding and shaking themselves, feeling for broken bones. While the horses cantered wildly away, Juno returned to her place on the lawn with a sense of duty fulfilled. Their examination concluded, the visitors got to their feet and made for the Hunt with the light of battle in their eyes.

'Hey!' the leader opened fire. 'What kind of a deal is this? Someone deliberately set that dawg on us.'

He had appeared to be generously built while seated, but was smaller than average standing up, his legs being unusually short. His jacket, vividly striped, was unbuttoned, exposing a T-shirt stamped with the words: Kiss me, I'm Irish. Again the Master was bereft of speech, and again it fell to Maguire to reply.

'Just her fun, mate,' he said. 'She wanted a bit of a lark.'

'That isn't so. One of you guys sicked her on. I'll take this further.'

'Do that. Out of earshot, if you're agreeable. This isn't a

ridin' school, you know, nor a circus neither.'

'Is that so? I thought it was, and you the ringmaster. But listen here, we haven't paid seventy-five bucks apiece to be insulted. The Tourist Board is going to hear about this.'

'Good. I dessay they're used to the likes of you. We're not,' said Maguire, unshaken. Then in a different tone of voice he continued, 'When you're ready, sir, shall we move off?'

'Eh? Oh yes, by all means. Time enough.'

'Don't know what the country is comin' to, sir,' Maguire said gravely, as the Hunt trotted on by the river bank. 'There was nothin' of this in the Major's day.' Settling his extraordinary hat more firmly on his head, he gave his whole attention to the matter in hand.

Francis had followed the scene with the greatest enjoyment and felt weak from holding his laughter in. Remembering his manners, he pulled himself together and tried to appease the ruffled sportsmen. They would have none of it, however, refusing the offer of drinks, of dry clothes for the victim of Toddy's mare, and of a conducted tour of the Castle, the leader observing that if he never saw a crummy old Irish ruin again it would be six months too soon. The suggestion of a lift to wherever they cared to go was likewise rejected; and their only concession was to leave the capture of their nags to the Castle groom, who could do what he liked with them.

'I'm through with Irish Ay-Ristocrats,' said he of the shirt, with a black look at Maguire. 'Circus, huh? I'll circus him. We'll get our money back and then some, see if we don't.'

With that they all marched away, uttering loud offensive comments for Francis to overhear.

Their blows, however, fell on space, for he was hurrying indoors to look for his wife. She had retired from the scene after Hilary Baggot's dig, dismayed by the sudden uncalled-for spite. Thus, while she was present for Maguire's dramatic appearance, she had missed the arrival of her compatriots and the knockabout farce set going by Juno. Francis, heroically, had decided not to mention this, for fear it upset her: at the back of his mind was a vague idea that Americans were all much the same, like Chinese; but he was aching to share the joke of Maguire's apotheosis.

He found her in the kitchen, studying a cookbook with an

air of perplexity. In the absence of Mrs Jeffars, she had taken on the duties of chef; for which nothing in previous life had prepared her. 'This book is written in double Dutch,' she complained. 'I'm doing a soufflé. The mix is ready, OK, flour, butter, grated cheese and yolks of eggs, like it said. But now I have to beat the egg-whites stiff and "fold in". What the heck does the woman mean? Fold in what?'

'Oh, four or eight, or something,' said Francis, gaily. 'Darling, what do you say to Maguire? That must have been what the old devil was at, when he yelled at me not to come up. Trying on the fancy dress!' And he went off in peals of merriment.

'What's so funny?' Marigold wished to know. 'If he was going to hunt at all, I guess he had to doll himself up like the others.'

'*Like the others!* Do you mean to say, you didn't notice anything strange?'

'I noticed plenty, but no more in Maguire than in anyone else.'

'No more? But his hat! and his jacket! dear God, his jacket! Like a Hungarian hussar! And his boots! And his gloves!'

'So that's why they all gawped at him, like he was crazy.'

'Well, partly that, and partly his turning out at all.'

'I must be very dumb, but I don't get the point. If he's good enough for them to meet here and drink his liquor, why isn't he good enough to ride with them?'

'Dear little democrat!' chuckled Francis, fondly.

'Who are you calling a Democrat?' cried Marigold with spirit. 'I'm a Republican. Do you imagine all Southerners are Democrats, just because of that grinning old Peanut Butter . . .'

'I wasn't referring to politics. All I meant . . .' Here he broke down again. 'You have to be a member of the Hunt, to start with,' he resumed when he could. 'You have to undergo various initiation rites and pay a subscription. It's enough to carry old Beaulieu off!'

'Just keeping a hundred hounds on the place and buying their food wouldn't count, of course.'

'You don't understand.'

'No. I'm sure I want to.'

'Darling, what's wrong with you?'

86

'Nothing. I just think there are some pretty nasty folks around.'

'Including me?'

'No, no, no!' she said, melting at once. 'I like Maguire, that's all. I like him a whole lot better than those starchy people out there.'

'Well then, you ought to wish he had stayed at home. He has never followed hounds before. He can ride, yes, Army fashion, but there's more to it than that.'

There was a pause, while Marigold vigorously beat the white of the eggs. Then she asked in a small voice: 'Francis, is it very risky, hunting?'

'Not really. Depends how you go and how good you are. No more risky than flying, and a whole lot safer than motoring in the west of Ireland.'

'Does it make people scary?' Marigold was very intent on her work.

'Not once they get going. A bit tense beforehand, probably. They say, if you don't want breakfast that morning, it's all right, but if you can't face dinner the evening before, you'd better give up.'

'You don't hunt,' Marigold said, beating away.

'I did, as a boy, but I just don't like it. Has someone told you, that's a sign of madness? But it's the hunting crowd, really. They think and talk of practically nothing else. In the summer, they fall into a kind of trance, and hardly speak at all.'

'I knew it was something like that!' Marigold exclaimed, wielding her whisk with such *élan* that some froth flew into her husband's eye. 'Well now, beat it. I must get on with this sofilé. It's going to take me from here until lunch to figure out what to do next.'

Meanwhile the Hunt was proceeding, and Maguire acquitting himself on the whole with credit. He made one mistake after another, but he did not ride over hounds and he kept his seat, besides showing pluck at fences and gates. One way and another, the Hunt decided he was a pretty good scout. His costume was assumed to be an elaborate device on the part of Francis, to make him look a fool; and Francis, they decided too, had encouraged the idea of his hunting at all, in the hope that he would break his neck.

87

# Chapter Twelve

Again the departure for Paris was put off. There were more allegations and threats against Juno, now with the Tourist Board behind them, and therefore not to be treated lightly. In this Land of a Thousand Welcomes, the awful things that people were used to stopped overnight, once a tourist was involved. The neighbourhood had been terrorized only last year by a string of young horses running wild, wrecking gardens and vegetable plots, smashing fences and forcing any who crossed their path to leap for the nearest ditch. As they belonged to a wealthy contractor with accomplices in the political world, it was taken for granted that nothing could ever be done; nor was it, until the day that, debouching from a boreen on to the high road, they caused a bus full of Yanks to collide with a lorry. Exactly what pressure was brought to bear, and by whom, was never made known, but the horses were up for auction the following week.

In reply to a telephone call from the Sergeant of Guards, Francis simply repeated his warning as to the fate of anyone touching a hair of Juno's head. It was not her fault, nor his, that these buffoons had invaded the Castle territory, and Bord Failte could jump in the river. Nevertheless, for the time being it seemed only prudent to stay where he was and protect her himself. Marigold was delighted, being more in love with Ireland every day, and more at home in the Castle; its only drawback in her eyes was that apparently against all tradition, it did not run to a ghost.

The point came up one morning as she chatted with Maguire. They were in the kitchen together, he cleaning and oiling a gun, she occupied with a new floral masterpiece, when a bloodcurdling howl from the regions below caused her to jump.

'What is that wonderful noise?' she asked, excitedly. 'I have heard it before. Surely, it must be a ghost?'

'Not it,' said Maguire, squinting down the shotgun's barrel, unmoved. 'That's natural, that is. Defective boiler.'

To him, a boiler that screamed like a soul in torment was indeed a part of natural life. The excellent repair in which, he had boasted to Francis, the house was kept was purely relative, to be seen against the decaying old mansions around. An air-lock in a pipe, for example, was dealt with at once, but the ancient plumbing system would growl, shriek or roar as the fancy took it. The lights all worked, even those in the great chandelier, but bells rang furiously of their own accord, for reasons that none could discover. What with this, and mysterious rumblings and creakings, and the moaning of wind in the chimneys, the place did often sound as if it were haunted from top to bottom and from end to end.

'A boiler! how disappointing,' Marigold sighed. 'I would have sworn it was some poor unquiet spirit, crying for help.'

'Catch a Barraclough makin' an 'orrible row like that,' Maguire reproved her. 'And the gentlemen mostly died over-seas, in a mill. Last thing they'd do, come back here, makin' theirselves a nuisance.'

'But it might have been a girl, a maid perhaps, who died for love of the handsome young heir!'

'I hope she'd know her place better than that,' Maguire said grimly. 'Them are nothin' but pishogues, ma'am.'

'What is a pishogue, Maguire?'

'A load of old codswallop, like these people are always talkin'. As for ghosts, I'll believe in 'em when I see one.'

'Not everyone *can* see them, you know,' said Marigold earnestly. 'The house could be swarming with them, all around us everywhere, and you and I not see a thing. But children always can, they say, and dogs as well.'

At this moment, as if on cue, Juno started to her feet with a growl and bared her teeth at some invisible presence.

'There!' exclaimed Marigold. 'She's probably seeing one now!'

Maguire threw a quick glance round, but recovered himself at once. 'Postman,' he said briefly. 'She heard his car pull up. Sit, Juno, there's a good lassie. None of your games today.'

With this further douche of cold water, he departed to take

89

in the letters. For all the sound commonsense of his replies, the conversation had left him uneasy. Ghosts swarming all round, that one one was able to see – what way to talk was that, for a nice young lady? Unhealthy, he called it, downright morbid; and he raised the matter anxiously with Francis when bringing his share of the post.

'Dead serious about it, too,' he added, shaking his head. 'It was that boiler set her off.'

'Well, if she wants a ghost, I suppose we must find her one,' said Francis. 'It might take her mind off those flower arrangements. Much more of them, and I shall be down with hay fever.'

All the same, he was ready with admiration and approval when Marigold appeared in her turn, staggering under the weight of the vase. It contained a phalanx of red-hot pokers, stiffly erect, rising from a profusion of mistletoe boughs.

'Lord Carrageen's Indian Summer,' she told him proudly. 'But have you a moment to spare? I want to talk to you about Maguire.'

'He's just been talking to me about you. It worries him, your believing in ghosts.'

'Is that a fact?' said Marigold, laughing. 'Well, listen now to what worries me. Right now he's cleaning one of your father's guns. He plans to go out with the others next week, for the shoot.'

Francis laughed delightedly, having foreseen this very event. 'Well, damn it, they'll be shooting his birds.'

'It's not that, but he's gone back to that tailor for some more of his dreadful clothes. At least, you say they are dreadful. Everyone will be sneering at him again.'

'Ah now, the tailor could hardly repeat a performance like that in one lifetime. He's a Jew boy from Belfast, and only here a month or two. He had never made, nor probably seen, hunting kit before, and used his imagination. This is different. He'll just make old Maguire look like a racing tout.'

'Still it seems to me, you shouldn't let him,' Marigold argued.

'And what d'you suggest I'm to do?'

'Well, there are closets full of tweeds that your father had.

Why couldn't I take something in for Maguire, the way I did for you at the funeral?'

Francis hesitated, far from pleased. Maguire as a comedy turn, acting lord of the manor, rejoiced his heart. The idea of Maguire in clothes that actually had been worn by his father was somehow distasteful. 'He mightn't agree,' he said finally. 'He clearly thought that gala rig was the very last word.'

'Sure. What the coloured people at home call, sharp dressing,' Marigold said, with a wise little nod. 'But they all go in for it there, and no one stands out.'

'What an angel you are,' he said fondly, and yet with half a sigh, as if angels were not altogether an unmixed blessing.

'That's a deal, then. Now what do you want for lunch?'

'You!' he said, making a sudden grab.

'Do be serious. I thought maybe . . . Francis, please!' For he had snatched her up and was striding purposefully in the direction of a sofa.

'I'm tired of being serious,' he panted. 'I want to bay the moon.'

'At eleven fifteen on a wet Monday morning!' she protested. 'What has the hour or the day or the weather to do with it? Are we like stupid hounds, who only bay the moon when they can see her? *La Lune est là, la lune est là, la lune est là*,' he carolled, depositing her on the sofa. 'Riding quietly above us in the heavens, although hidden from our view. Our homage will be all the sweeter to her on that account . . .' But now the flow was brought to a sudden end. 'Oh good morning, Rector,' he said lamely. 'I didn't hear you come in.'

Dr Thornton was looking down at them with gentle surprise and concern. 'I trust my call is not untimely,' he remarked with an air of solicitude. 'No doubt I should have telephoned first.'

'Not at all, by no means. We were only discussing what we wanted for lunch.'

'New England Boiled Dinner,' Marigold put in, by way of further clarification. 'I must really get on with it.' Pink and dishevelled, she hurried out of the room.

'Please sit down,' said Francis, smoothing his hair and straightening his tie, and trying to keep the irritation out of his voice. It was the familiar pattern of Irish life: were you expecting a visitor, he came, if at all, hours late: when you wanted to enjoy yourself in peace, someone was sure to bob up, the devil only knew whence and why. 'What can I do for you?'

'Well . . . By the way, I was so grieved to hear of your accident, although it is delightful to have you with us still. I trust there have been no lasting effects?'

'Not to me, anyhow. It was Carrageen in the car.'

'Lord Carrageen? Dear me, I heard . . . one scarcely knows what to . . . Lord Carrageen! Bless my soul.'

For a minute or two there was silence, while he struggled to arrange his thoughts. Like Francis, he was the victim just then of a curious disposition of Irish life, namely, that whatever was put forward in jest, to be chuckled over as entirely absurd, was sooner or later bound to come true. His story was so odd that he hardly knew where to begin; and when at last he took the plunge, it sounded odder than ever.

For several Sundays past, Maguire had been attending St Andrew's church and occupying the Barraclough pew. There could be no real objection to this, although Dr Thornton had always assumed – uncharitably, as he saw now – that the man was a papist. But yesterday, after Morning Prayer, he had come round to the vestry before the Rector had even disrobed, and offered to read the Lessons in future.

'I say, offered,' said Dr Thornton, 'but that perhaps is not quite the word. Rather, he seemed to express his intention of doing so. And not only that. He looked keenly about him as he spoke, and drew his finger along one of the shelves, examining the dust it collected with an air of marked disapproval. I am only too conscious of all that needs to be done but, kind as the ladies are, it is as much as they can do to clean the church itself and keep the graveyard in some kind of order.'

'He is beginning to feel his oats, all right,' said Francis. 'You heard about him riding to hounds?'

'Yes, indeed, but if I may say so, the Hunt is one thing and Divine Service another.'

'But why not let old Maguire have a go? He couldn't sound worse than the BBC.'

'No, certainly not,' Dr Thornton agreed with a shudder. 'But the dilemma goes beyond that of mere diction. How can

I ask Colonel Beaulieu, a churchwarden for so many years, to stand down in favour of . . . of . . .'

'The apostles were hardly out of the top drawer,' said Francis, with a mocking smile.

'Quite true, very true, but that was some time ago. And they were not in Ballinaween. When I raised the point at our vestry meeting last night, there was such dissension as threatened to split the parish in two. Certain people – I mention no names – supported Maguire, for worthy reasons, excellent reasons, no doubt, while others, equally worthy and good, said if I allowed this to happen they would worship elsewhere. A veritable schism !'

How, Francis wondered, had this shepherd so devotedly tended his flock all these years and discovered so little about them? By now, they had dwindled to a mere twenty-three: they should have clung together, surrounded by popish hordes as they were. Instead, they were perpetually feuding, dissenting and kicking up trouble. The vestry meeting was not divided on the point at issue, but had merely seen the chance of a fine old scrap. Worship elsewhere, indeed ! In Ballinaduff, perhaps? where the Rector was the new type of person, a shop-keeper's son, with a brogue you could cut with a knife? Or at the next parish after that, where the incumbent was English, High Church and a pansy?

'They would never do it, Rector,' he assured him. 'There's far too much to keep them here !'

'It is kind of you to say that,' was the doleful reply. 'But I confess to finding myself altogether in the dark. Leaving the views of the parish out of it, the attitude of Maguire himself is a puzzle. I naturally put a few questions about his baptism and so forth, and he could tell me nothing. He said that when he joined the Army, they asked him what his religion was and he told them, none at all: whereupon they wrote him down as C. of E.'

'Their usual practice, I believe.'

'Only too sadly probable,' the Rector concurred, shaking his head. 'But he is not in the Army now. What has brought him so unexpectedly into our fold? In a way, of course, it is a matter for rejoicing, but on the other hand . . . Suppose that Colonel

Beaulieu declines to surrender his place?' He broke off here, appalled by a sudden vision of an unseemly struggle between the pair to gain control of the lecturn.

'I thought you said that Beaulieu's heart was not altogether in the business?'

'That is unfortunately so, and matters are worse now that hunting is on. His mind is apt to wander away, and there are long uncomfortable pauses . . .'

'I think that may be the answer,' said Francis. 'Maguire wants everything carried out smartly, as if life were a form of drill. He intended to reorganize the whole estate on military lines, but I managed to talk him out of it.'

'Could you not talk him out of this notion as well?' the Rector pleaded earnestly. 'I cannot see the Colonel taking it quietly, however little he cares for the duty itself. And, frankly, I should be on his side. No doubt I am a very poor Christian, but I would as soon appoint a lady.'

Francis promised to do what he could, but he did not feel very sanguine. 'I cannot make head or tail of the chap, to be honest,' he said.

'I can make head or tail of nothing these days,' the poor Rector responded, and wearily took his departure.

# Chapter Thirteen

'I was thinking about Maguire,' said Marigold in deep contrition. The New England Boiled Dinner had been flavoured with sugar instead of salt.

'Everyone seems to be thinking of him just now,' said Francis, wry-faced, taking a pull at his wine.

'That Boiled Dinner is one of the great dishes of the world, according to my cookbook,' his wife went on. 'I did hope you would enjoy it. They don't have all the ingredients here that were mentioned, corned brisket, pickled pork, bay leaves, horse radish, stuff like that, but I made do with onions and potatoes and mutton chops.'

'But for the sugar, then, it would have been our exquisite national standby, Irish Stew. Tell you what, shall we borrow the car and get a meal outside? Your cooking improves by leaps and bounds, but has some little way to go before one could eat it.'

'Another crack out of you, and I'll bring on the dessert !'

But the prospect of a drive and food prepared by someone else was appealing. Francis was ready with an idea as to where they could go. Report had it, there was a restaurant newly opened beside the Shannon airport with a superb Italian chef, to which people now were flocking from near and far. It put the London Ritz to shame: a French hotelier had offered the chef a fortune to leave: top rating was promised for the next edition of a leading guide. Marigold always marvelled at the extent of her husband's information, as he never spoke to anyone much, and she was carried away by this example of it.

Maguire consented at once to their having the car, on condition that Juno went as well: there was, he said, a visitor coming that she might not care for the looks of. He was so emphatic on the point, and so plainly eager for them to vanish too, that they suspected she would not have been alone in this.

The rain had stopped by now and the country was innocently

beaming in the sun, as if this were its normal state and anything else, a mirage. The tawny bog was studded with little
pools reflecting the blue of the sky or the stolid faces of cattle,
staring down at them apparently deep in thought. They and a
few curly-horned rams were the only living creatures passed
for mile upon mile: the two young people in the car had a
sense, familiar in rural Ireland, of being alone in the world.

'What did the Rector want, by the way?' Marigold asked
after a while. 'Goodness, your Irish habits!' She could not get
used to people walking into the house as if they lived there. 'A
nice fool I felt! I wonder what he made of it all.'

'Nothing much, I think. He was too full of his own worries.'

Marigold was able to shed some light on these, as Maguire
talked more to her than to anyone else. His mother was newly
dead and, although he had never cared for her, a proper old
vixen and Nosey Parker, he thought it only decent to turn out
for church parade, anyhow once, to mark the occasion. But he
was so shocked at what he saw and heard, not merely by the
Colonel's performance but by the unearthly wails from Miss
Hackle's harmonium, by the hymn numbers on the board at
variance with those the Rector gave out, by the feeble ragged
singing itself and by the omission of 'God Save the Queen' at
the end, that he returned on the following Sunday, to check if
it were equally bad. It was, if anything, worse: the Colonel
had a cold and frequently used his handkerchief with the blare
of an irate elephant, the Rector had forgotten his spectacles
and preached confusedly off the cuff, one of the three choir
boys incessantly scratched his behind, another, his head.
Punishment drill for the lot, was what Maguire would have
liked to award: this being impossible, he continued his attend-
ance as a regular thing while planning how he might shake
them. The demotion of the Colonel was but the first of various
reforms he had in mind.

'Civil war, I foresee,' said Francis. 'No wonder the Boiled
Dinner came to grief.'

'Oh, it wasn't just that. I asked him about your father's
tweeds, and you were quite wrong, Francis, he was really
touched. He said he only wished I had spoken before, it was
too late now, the tailor had some all but ready. Two knicker-

96

bocker suits! He showed me patterns of the material, and they were quite something. A dog's tooth in red, black and white, and a plaid in salmon, green and blue. Wait till you see them!'

Francis secretly licked his lips at the prospect. 'But he can just hang them up in the press and leave them there,' he pointed out, humanely. 'Who's to know?'

'That's the difficulty. The tailor would. He's going along.'

'Maguire has asked Rabinovitch to the shoot?'

'Not exactly. Rabinovitch asked himself. He is hoping to book some orders from the County. Now, Francis, why do you have to laugh like that?'

Francis was laughing so wildly that he had to pull in to the verge and stop. It was fortunate that he did, as another vehicle was now approaching, not driven really fast but ambling from side to side as if it had the road to itself. Inside, at the wheel, was Lord Carrageen, his left hand exploring the person of a buxom wench, with a mop of flame-red curls, whose resistance appeared to be of a half-hearted nature.

'Will you take your crub away out of that, you bold thing!' a delighted squeal came floating through the car window.

Intent on his work, Lord Carrageen had no eyes for anything else, and Francis hooted just in time to avert a calamity. As it was, the Marina got off with a dented wing and a yard or so of scratched paint. 'Damn silly place to park!' the aggressor grumbled. 'Might have caused an accident. Hullo, Mrs Marigold,' he went on, more pleasantly. 'Meet Rosie O'Malley!'

But Miss O'Malley was adjusting her skirt with her nose in the air and did not wish to be met.

'Shy,' his lordship explained. 'Well, off we go. Mind where you stop, in future. You youngsters are all the same, think of nobody but yourselves.'

Francis got out of the car to assess the damage. 'It could have been worse, I suppose,' he remarked. 'At least, this time, I shan't have to buy a new one. Well, the old rip seems to have struck oil at last. Wonder where he found it.'

They had barely covered a mile when a red-faced man in the usual veteran Morris Minor signalled to them to stop again. 'Did ye pass a car back the road, with an auld man in it?' he shouted urgently. 'And a young lady with him too?'

97

'We did,' Francis sang out. 'But it was a while ago, on the Mallow Road.'

'And was it thravellin' fast?'

'Like the wind! Must be an elopement,' he chuckled, moving on, 'and that, the outraged father – or fiancé. They don't marry young round here.'

'Why, Francis Hugh Barraclough, and I always thought you honest!' said Marigold gravely. 'You deliberately sent that poor fellow astray.'

'Mallow is a charming spot. He can drown his sorrows there as well as anywhere else,' said Francis. 'And we must stick by our own, after all.'

'The class hang-ups you people have!' Marigold said, with indulgent superiority. 'And are you as good as that lord?' she teased him.

'Well, yes. That is, yes and no. If he should marry the fruit in his car, she would go in to dinner ahead of you.'

'I don't know if I should care for that,' Marigold said, after a pause.

'I am quite sure that you wouldn't,' he told her, smiling.

After that a silence fell, as the pangs of hunger began to gnaw. To leave the kitchen clear for Maguire, who breakfasted off gargantuan fries of blood puddings, eggs and bacon, they contented themselves with coffee and toast in the morning; but the strong air of the west gave them the appetite of wolves for even an early lunch, and it was now going on for two o'clock.

'Darling, do leave me alone,' said Francis crossly, his eyes on the road, driving flat out. 'I love you madly – but *please*!'

'For heaven's sake!' cried Marigold, roused from a dream of steak *béarnais*. 'When did I ever act like that?'

Tired of playing gooseberry in the back, Juno had pushed her great head forward and was passionately licking her master's ear.

'Sorry, sorry, sorry. Lie down, you bitch, or I'll slay you.'

By the time they got to Shannon he was beginning to think there might be worse things in life than sugary Boiled Dinner. Identifying the famous restaurant by the newness of the building and the flags of many nations fluttering bravely above it, they pulled up and leapt out without bothering to lock or even shut the doors of the car. To their dismay, however, the entrance was guarded by a few obese mop-haired youths who declined to let them in. A few weary travellers gazed with longing through the plate-glass windows at a number of men, similar to the guard but stouter and shaggier, who were seated at a long banqueting table and guzzling away as if they had starved for a week. Waiters hovered round them, filling their glasses and piling their plates with a respectful care remote from normal Irish practice.

'What's all this?' demanded Francis. 'You can't be shut. It's barely half-past two.'

'Strike on,' growled one of the men, who appeared to be in charge. 'Industrial dispute.'

'What's it about?' Francis snapped.

'That's confidential,' the picket replied, with an air of importance.

'And what are those fellows doing inside?'

'Them's the Action Committee,' said the man. 'Clear off now, will you?'

'Is the airport restaurant open?'

'It is not,' said the wretch with nasty glee. 'They all came out in sympathy with us. And the snack bar's cleaned out, hours ago. You'll not get a crumb, without you take the plane to Ameriky.'

This brililant thrust caused the group to burst into noisy laughter, while its author smiled his acknowledgement and Francis ground his teeth.

'Seems that Ireland is just like any other place, after all,' said Marigold piteously.

In the next moment, however, she was proved wrong. The braying mirth died down as quickly as it had broken out, and the faces of the militants took on an expression of ludicrous fear. Juno had quietly left the car and joined the party, and was surveying them all attentively, looking from one to the other as if considering which to deal with first.

'Stay perfectly still, and you'll be all right,' Francis advised them. 'She is a nice character, but staunchly conservative. Come on, darling, in we go.'

They seated themselves at a table near the door, while the

picket hastily re-formed outside as the indignant travellers endeavoured to rush it. One of the waiters came running up.

'Dogs not allowed,' he panted. 'Anyway, I cannot serve you.'

'Hear that, Juno?' Francis purred. 'Dogs not allowed, and the gentleman cannot serve us.'

Juno exposed her teeth and, to dispel any possible doubt of her sincerity, accompanied the act with a soft but menacing growl.

'Would he go near me?' quavered the menial, taking a few steps backward.

'Not if you bring us food at once,' Francis assured him. 'We will have whatever the Action Committee is eating, it smells very good. And a bottle of Fleurie, while we're about it. I wonder,' he continued pensively, as the waiter scurried off, his archless feet turning out like those of a penguin, 'how the Irish got their name for reckless physical courage?'

'Or for lovely manners,' Marigold sighed. 'We could almost have been in Paris.'

The Committee meanwhile were throwing glances at them and muttering. Now a member jumped up and darted from the room in pursuit of the waiter.

'Don't say he's going to countermand your order?' Marigold wailed.

'I rather think not. We shouldn't like that at all, Juno, should we?'

Presently, along with a loaded tray of chicken, pork, turnips, potatoes, tipsy cake, Fairygold cheese, rolls and butter, cups of greyish coffee and the bottle of wine, steaming from a quick plunge into hot water, the waiter in fact brought a conciliatory message from the Committee Chairman. 'Mick says, would you eat up as fast as you can?' he gasped, hurriedly placing the viands before them. 'This is highly irregular. If the crowd in the kitchen knew, they'd be calling us scabs and blacklegs. And if annywan should question you, you've to tell 'em you're foreign press. There's no charge, be the way. Company's compliments!'

'But what are they striking about?' Francis asked again.

'Isn't that personal, and just for themselves,' the waiter reproved him.

'Surely the Press has a right to know.'

But the waiter quelled him with a look and hastened back to his other duties.

As often happens in Ireland, the men had struck because they felt so inclined, and had not formulated their reasons as yet. There were ample grounds to choose from, a man ticked off for being constantly late, another for dropping a brillo pad in a fricasee, a notice in the convenience requiring personnel to wash their hands after use, another in the kitchen announcing that thefts of food would lead to dismissal, one provocative insult after another. It would probably all boil down to a general complaint of inhuman conditions, but for the moment they were simply having a high old time. Their meal at last concluded, they drank an amazing number of toasts and finally, such as were able to stand did so and burst into a moving exhortation to 'Arise, ye starvelings of the gutter!'

'Well, really!' chuckled Marigold. 'I don't know where I saw so many barrel-bellies at one time together!'

'Hush, keep your voice down. If they suspect they're being laughed at, I doubt even Juno could save us.'

All were too busy howling their anthem to entertain suspicions of any kind whatever. The young couple waited politely for them to finish it before rising to leave, and were saluted with a waving of clenched fists and jovial cries of Good Luck! and, Up the Workers! The picket was also in friendly mood by now and greeted them with fraternal smiles. Among the besieging travellers, since called away to their flight, were the Yankee tourists who had aspired to go a-hunting with the Ballinaduff and Charlotteville, and now were shaking the dust of Ireland from their feet, as they hoped, for ever. Recognizing Francis, they had furiously wished to know why a servant from Castle Reef was made a special and privileged case; and were told that domestic workers were the victims of exploitation, too, and accordingly comrades and brothers.

'Why didn't ye tell us who you were?' the picket leader inquired of Francis with gentle reproach. 'We'd have let you through like a shot.'

'All snobs at heart, I fear,' said Francis complacently, as he

101

and Marigold went their way. 'I wonder how on earth he knew.'

Marigold was busy with thoughts of her own. 'You told me the chef here was Italian and a genius,' she said.

'Just another little Irish folk tale. I should have known better. You seemed to tuck in manfully, all the same.'

'Sure. They ate roasted rats in Paris, 1870. But no one said it was *haute cuisine.*'

They went on to the airport and hung about awhile, not wishing to appear at the Castle before Maguire had dealt with his mysterious caller. With the flair of American women, Marigold made like a homing bird for the gift shop, where she bought a cut-glass decanter, a model fishing-boat and a hunting horn. Francis went to the bookstall, where she found him later, smiling broadly over the *Irish Press.*

'Two IRA lads have blown themselves up,' he informed her. 'One short week after their triumphant acquittal by the Special Court in Dublin.'

'And you're amused at that!' she cried, staring at him.

'No, my sweet. I am tickled by the buffoonery of the race. And, yes, I am smiling too to think of the people those bombs were intended for. They might have been dead, crippled or blind by now, without this national gift for balling things up. So let's have no mourning for that pair or, much as I love you, I might get rather cross.'

'I can't but think it is all most terribly sad. How do they get that way?'

'They don't. They always were. Now, if you are sure there is nothing else you need buy to make yourself happy, we could move towards home.'

They drove most of the distance without a word, their minds full of separate matters. Francis was wondering, not by any means for the first time, why he still believed a single word that was ever spoken. The marvellous dream of the restaurant, the gruesome reality of it, were of a pattern familiar to him since boyhood. No end of imagination, but of rather inferior quality, he mused: ideal for the art of propaganda, in which this people undoubtedly led the world. Marigold was still reflecting sadly on the boys who had blown themselves to bits.

'I thought it only went on in the North,' she said at last, as they were approaching the Castle, tranquil and fairylike in the fading afternoon sun.

'Um? Oh, that. Well yes, that is where the atrocities usually happen. Not always though, there have been incidents. And down here are the arsenals, the factories and hide-outs. It is so delightfully safe, in comparison.'

'One never hears about it.'

'You never do, about things that really matter here. But everyone knows about them.'

# Chapter Fourteen

Mr Aloysius Quirke, solicitor, left the Castle feeling on top of the world. It was only the second time in his life that he had got his foot through the door. The first was that dinner party, at which Mr Francis and his friends had snubbed and high-hatted him, made him feel a person of no account. Today he was there in the capacity of legal adviser to its rightful lord, and young Barraclough's nose was nicely out of joint. He felt like one who takes a fortress singlehanded and runs his flag up on the tower. His father, God rest him, a cattleman as Mr Goodchild had surmised, had made repeated but unsuccessful attempts to dispose of his crocks to the agent. His grand-mammy, God rest her, had been a kitchen maid until her pilfering and breakages began to tower above the accepted norm. And here was he, Looshie, being ushered out of the front door by the master of it all in person!

'There'll be an inven*tory* somewhere or other,' he said, by way of a farewell tip. 'Mr Francis will know where it is, don't let him cod you he doesn't. You'll need to look out for your own.'

His conquest of Maguire had gone more smoothly than he dared to hope. A first meeting had been arranged by the tailor Rabinovitch, who occupied premises owned by Looshie and was falling behind with the rent. Maguire had not by any means taken to him at once. The man was scruffy, greasy, physically B3 and a poor type altogether. But Looshie knew his onions and immediately struck a note sure of response from an Army chap accustomed to order, method and the Queen's Regulations.

'I'll bet you found a shocking mess up at the Big House,' he said genially. 'These old families! Half the time they don't even know what they've got. One of my clients had to sell up and the auctioneer came on a silver box in an attic that he thought looked pretty nice. Jewels stuck round it and that. Just lying there, full of odds and ends, black as pitch. We had it valued in Dublin, and it was worth two thousand pounds!'

The auctioneer had withdrawn the box from sale and acquired it himself for a hundred and fifty, but Looshie was too much the artist to overload a narrative with details. He continued in jocular vein, his hard little eyes noting the effect of every word on Maguire.

'Another lad on my books,' he said, 'was skint till he couldn't mend a door or a window-pane, so he said. The rain coming in at his bedroom annoyed him, and didn't he keep it out with a painting by some old geezer, Stubbs I think the name was, that turned out was a masterpiece? And there's how they go.'

After a few more anecdotes of the kind, Maguire had invited Looshie to visit the Castle for a recce, in case similar treasures were lying about for the taking; and this was what had occupied the pair that afternoon.

Looshie's departing car met the Marina in the avenue, and Francis gave a whistle. 'Now what?' he groaned.

He was not long in finding out, as Maguire requested a private discussion the moment he entered the hall. Looshie had learned with delight that, beside the military sense of order he had expected, there was in Maguire a fund of greed and the habit of chronic suspicion. Francis was now to learn, with dismay, that there was no expelling ideas from his head once they had taken hold, nor any chance of getting new ones in.

'What's all this about an inventory, Maguire?' he asked, bewildered. 'There never has been one, as far as I know, and why should there be? We have no heirlooms, nothing entailed. If my father wished to give away or sell anything here, he was free to do so. You, on the other hand, own the chattels for your lifetime merely, and may not dispose of a single one. So what would be the point of listing them?'

This speech he made several times without producing the slightest impression. 'All very well, Mr Francis,' Maguire kept on saying darkly, 'but I must look to my own.'

'I imagine you got that phrase from Quirke,' said Francis. 'Well, go ahead and look to it. No one will stop you.'

'That's more than I know,' Maguire said. 'What about the family jewels? Mr Quirke mentioned a di'mond tye-ara and all. We was looking high and low and found no trace.'

'Of course you didn't, they are in the Bank and no concern of yours. That much I can tell you,' said Francis shortly.

'How do you know?' Maguire rounded on him.

'I asked Mr Goodchild to make inquiries.'

'Ah. And I'll get Mr Quirke to make some more. I shall want to hear when them jewels were deposited.'

'Are you suggesting I sneaked off with them and made the deposit myself?' said Francis, laughing in spite of his irritation.

'I'm not suggestin' nothin',' retorted Maguire. 'But I must look to my own.'

There was no piercing the fog in that brain: Looshie had done his work too well.

After some careful thought, Maguire determined to make an inventory for himself. It could then be matched against the existing one that sooner or later Mr Francis would be obliged to cough up. He would go methodically through the house, room by room, from the lobby between the front door and the hall to the last and barest attic. No sooner was the decision made than he set to work. 'Stand, umbrellas and walkin' sticks for the use of', the document began: 'barometer, one, table, one with silver salver, visittin' cards for collection of, one . . .' But it all went very slowly. Once he had finished the lobby and started on the hall, he realized that apart from military relics he had no idea how most of the stuff should be described. By Wednesday lunchtime he was still only halfway through the drawing-room and, furthermore, he was in a state of mental confusion that posed a threat to his plans; and, his programme being a full one, he reluctantly threw in the towel. For on Sunday, there was the Lessons to read and serious things to discuss with the Rector after church: on Monday, there was the shoot; and on Tuesday, the third of November, he would be crossing over to London for various regimental larks and reunions, culminating in the celebration of Remembrance Sunday, which the Major and he had never missed. To make sure, however, of things going forward in his absence, he decided to pay a visit to Mr Quirke.

Looshie listened to all he had to say and expressed strong

disapproval of young Barraclough's attitude. After burying his face in his hands awhile, as if in pious meditation, he rang up Mr Goodchild. On behalf of his client, Mr Maguire of Castle Reef, he said, he would be glad to know where the Barraclough jewels were.

'Why?' asked Mr Goodchild, curtly.

'To ascertain the date of lodgement.'

'Well, of all . . .' Mr Goodchild gasped. Then, with an effort, he said, 'I will put you through to Mr Twigg.'

'Why so? I have nothing to do with Twigg,' Looshie replied. 'You represented the family when you came down. Am I to understand, the jewels were deposited since?'

The sounds that travelled along the wire suggested that Mr Goodchild's breath was giving him trouble again. After a while he managed to say, 'Major Barraclough lodged them with the Bank himself, shortly after his wife's decease.'

'Which Bank, will you tell me? I shall need to verify that.'

'Good day to you, sir !' The receiver went down.

Looshie was well pleased with the result of this call. He knew that Goodchild spoke the truth and, had he supplied the information desired, there would have been the end of it. Now he could apply for a Court direction which, leading nowhere, nevertheless would push up the costs and with luck get into the papers. He explained to Maguire what an order of discovery was, in legal phrases that passed over that wooden head but left its owner feeling he was in the very best of hands.

The minute he was alone once more, Looshie rang up Francis.

'Me client has instructed me to get a valuer in,' he lied. 'I take it, you would have no objection?'

'What your client really needs, is a strait jacket,' was the crushing reply. 'First an inventory, now a valuation . . . You know the terms of my father's will, no doubt?'

Looshie did indeed, and fairly revelled in the phantom case he was building on them. Carrageen himself, that impetuous litigant, had never been cajoled into anything half as flimsy. 'Those are me instructions,' he repeated.

'I daresay. But isn't it a lawyer's duty to stop his client making an ass of himself and throwing his money about?

107

Maguire can't dispose of anything here, so what earthly difference does the value of it make to him?'

'You and I can see that, of course,' said Looshie, in a man of the world kind of way. 'But me client is a simple fellow, and he wants to know what he's worth.'

'Well, there must be insurance policies somewhere, here or with Goodchild. He could get an inkling from those.'

'No, he wants to know exactly what the value of everything is, each picture, piece of silver, carpet, chest of drawers. He never owned a penny above his soldier's pay before. It's only natural, if it's gone to his head a little. And don't forget, he comes of an oppressed people, with a long history of sorrow, injustice and famine behind him, Francis.' Looshie wound up, with a tremor in his voice.

'Bosh, Mr Quirke. His father was a soldier and batman to a great-uncle of mine, as he himself was to my father. As for the long sad history prior to that, I know nothing about it and nor do you. I'm beginning to think you're a bit of a rascal.'

Looshie was deeply hurt by the imputation. 'Ah now . . .' he began in a plaintive tone; but Francis had already rung off.

The next thing was that Maguire started prowling about the Castle like the unquiet spirit of Marigold's fancy. Small objects he carried off to his lair and hoarded, as squirrels hoard their nuts. Larger ones he would study awhile with a bemused sort of air before drifting off and hurriedly doubling back, as if he expected to find someone in the act of removing them. He tied the handles of drawers together to prevent their opening and sealed the doors of the principal rooms; he barricaded the mouths of the main passages with pieces of furniture and set up a chain of booby traps, into which now and then he stumbled himself. The pleasant relations of earlier times were ended and, if he met Francis or Marigold on his rounds, he turned abruptly away.

'Is it the full moon coming?' Marigold wondered. 'Does it affect him, the way it affects the hounds?'

'Or is he expanding, as the universe itself is supposed to be? Perhaps, like it, he will suddenly burst one day,' Francis replied, shaking his head. 'It's devilish uncomfortable, whatever it is. But we'll have to try and humour him.'

When, however, late on Saturday afternoon, Maguire broke his long silence with a request for the key of the strong-box, Francis flatly refused it.

'Still after the jewels? There's nothing in the box but old family papers. Pick it up and shake it, and you'll realize that.'

Maguire had already done so and concluded that among them would be a note as to where the jewels were lodged or even a map as to where they were buried.

'We'll see what Mr Quirke has to say,' he growled.

'By all means. Another ten or twenty pounds on his bill will hardly annoy him.'

'It's you'll have to pay the bill when you lose.'

'Dear God! Lose what?' Francis felt his brain beginning to reel. 'Quirke or no Quirke, you won't get that key.'

Maguire flung angrily out of the room, and a few minutes later Francis heard him shouting to Juno to come for a walk.

Marigold was in one of the barns, preparing a Hallowe'en party for a troop of local children. With the house to himself, Francis thought he would make a tour of inspection, to study Maguire's doings in detail. In the long annals of the Barraclough family, there could have been nothing like this. Reef had always stood there, a firm orderly clearing in the jungle, and now the jungle was breaking in. Or, rather, it had been deliberately invited in by his own dear father, with the best intentions in the world. That excellent man had entertained no illusions about the people except for one, very commonly found in the Big Houses: he believed that his own servants were somehow 'different', that they were devoted and loyal. The Goodchilds of the country knew much better.

At the moment, as so often, the electricity men were working to rule and the wan light of their normal production had faded to a dull orange flicker. The Castle was eerie enough as it was, with the bells ringing, rats scuttling and from time to time the boiler below giving vent to its bloodchilling howl. It was a perfect Hallowe'en, to be sure: the darkening sky must be full of witches, the shadowy corridors aswarm with presences not of this earth.

Gingerly Francis made his way along them, marvelling at the fortifications thrown up by Maguire. You would have thought the man was expecting an onslaught by the *jacquerie* at the very least. He was clearly as mad as the March Hare, and a splendid joke. But when the young man reached his father's bedroom, he was suddenly not amused. Here too the door had been sealed with tape and wax, warning him, the son, to keep outside.

He ripped the fastening off at once and went into the room. Everything was in order, in its usual place, the bed made up, towels on the washstand, hairbrushes in line along the dressing-table as if at any moment the Major might return and wish to use them. The room itself was somehow alive, waiting, holding its breath.

Slowly, Francis walked across to one of the massive wardrobes and opened it. It contained a number of uniforms that his father had worn, from his Sandhurst days to his retirement, simple cadet to fullblown Major, everyday kit and ceremonial, all in a neat long row, the early ones slim and spare, the rest growing steadily larger. Why his father had conserved all these, Francis had never understood; they were not medals or trophies, but mere cast-offs that signified nothing. He now took one of them from its peg, the cadet-passing-out-with-Sword-of-Honour and, slipping his outer clothes off, tried it on. It fitted as if it were made for him and, surveying the effect in the wardrobe glass, he could not help thinking it suited him too.

So, at his age, the burly florid man he remembered must have looked: it was the past that stood there, gazing back at him from the mirror. And it was also the might-have-been for himself, if he had not broken away. But he would not have been as his father was, all was changed and upside down. He would have been no more than a mercenary, fighting for rabble against other rabble. A phrase his nurse would use when he went too far as a child came into his mind: I think we've come to the place called Stop. That was where the Barracloughs had come to, and now the world belonged to Maguire.

Above all, in the might-have-been, he would never have come across Marigold; and at the very idea of that everything else went out of his head. Marigold!! He would go to her immediately and show himself in this dashing outfit: how the

110

dear romantic soul would love it! Fastening on the Sword of Honour, he squared his shoulders and set off at a dignified pace for the barn.

Cap. 2

Marigold meanwhile was doing the best she could by the light of some battered old paraffin lamps. Earlier, she had laboriously festooned the barn with ropes of many-coloured electric bulbs, only to find when the work was completed that no current was laid on there, frills of that nature being reserved for horses and hounds. In semi-darkness she had to set up a trestle-table for the baskets of apples and nuts and the dishes of buttered barmbrack slices, bury small treasures in a barrel of sawdust and fill a tub with water for bob-apple; and she was now at work on a coconut shy. The faint glow of the lamps produced an authentic hallowe'en atmosphere, but it sure was creepy too: she was wondering if the children would be scared and if she might not have been so herself at their age.

Then all at once in rushed Maguire, his eyes wide with horror, and seized her roughly by the arm.

'Mrs Francis, ma'am, the Major is back!' he gasped out incoherently. 'The Major is walkin'! I seen him, no mistake, just as he was all them years ago. Came through the haggard, I did, and there he was, marchin' slow towards me, sword on and all, no hat, moon on his face, a-smilin' to hisself like there was something he knew that tickled him. And movin' this way!'

'Maguire, I'm afraid you've been drinking,' Marigold said with composure, and continued her work as if he had not spoken. 'Help me fix these coconuts if you can, the party is due to begin.'

'No, ma'am, not a drop, I swear! Me and Mr Francis had words again about the property and I took the dog out, to cool off like, and I was just coming back when I saw – It!' Maguire shuddered. 'Saw it plain as plain. Plain as I see you now.'

'How very odd,' she remarked, with the same provoking calm. 'I thought you didn't believe in ghosts!'

'I said I'd believe in 'em when I saw one and now I have. And this is their night. And he's after me. What have I done, to call him up? I only looked for what was mine . . . Oh, don't you go out, Mrs Francis!' For Marigold, with no time to spare for argument, was going towards the door with the idea of inspecting the phenomenon for herself. 'Don't leave me to him, don't leave me alone!'

'If there's a ghost around, I plan to see it,' she answered cheerfully. 'I always wanted to, and didn't I say there should be one, knocking about in a place like this?' She walked coolly out of the barn and in the next moment the trembling Maguire heard a peal of laughter, followed by the words: 'Francis, you dope, for heaven's sake, what are you playing at now?'

'Am I not a sight for sore eyes?' a well known voice responded complacently.

'You all but frightened Maguire to death.'

'Surely not, surely not. How could that be?' Francis appeared in the barn doorway and regarded his victim with amusement. 'He does look rather shaken. Is this the hero who saved my father's life under a hail of bullets? What can have been the cause?'

'I thought you *was* your father,' muttered Maguire, acutely embarrassed and struggling to regain his poise. 'Dressin' yourself up in his togs! You had no call.'

'Must be, the tape on his bedroom door set me off,' said Francis drily. 'There was certainly no call for that. Be off, Maguire. Begone. I don't think I wish to see you.'

'Nor me you neither,' retorted Maguire, flaring up. 'That was a soddy trick to play, you done it a-purpose. I might have known it couldn't of been the Major, he was a gent. I'm off, all right. I'll go to England this very night and . . . and make me wishes known from there!'

He stumbled away, swearing and threatening under his breath.

'Just help me fix these goddam nuts, they keep falling out of their sockets,' Marigold said. 'If there wasn't trouble enough without ghosts and tantrums!'

Shortly afterwards the children started to trickle in, dressed up to the nines, and for the next couple of hours their hosts had their hands full, encouraging shy little girls, seeing that everyone got his share and intervening in battles between the boys. When the guests had departed and the pair got back to the house, there was no sign of Maguire and the car had gone: he had, seemingly, made good his threat.

'He was going across next week anyway,' Francis said. 'How relieved the Rector will be!'

'Did you really dress up like that to scare him?'

'Of course not, never entered my head. I wanted to give you a delightful surprise.'

'He sure is a crackpot,' Marigold sighed. 'But I still can't but like him.'

'Let's not think about him,' Francis proposed. 'Lately, we have thought about him far too much. There must be other matters to occupy our minds.'

Here, he spoke more accurately than he knew. Very soon there were matters to occupy not only their minds but those of everyone in the neighbourhood and throughout the country at large. Before they went to bed, Marigold switched on the wireless to get the time and happened to do so just as a special announcement was given out. Lord Carrageen had been kidnapped in the course of the evening, and a splinter group of the Irish Patriot Front was claiming responsibility.

# Chapter Fifteen

The group in question was called the Progressive, or Prog, to distinguish it from the seven or eight other groups that had splintered off the IPF, itself a splinter from one of the two main factions within the Movement. All of these avowed a single aim, the unity of Ireland, and employed similar methods in their struggle to achieve it, so that strangers were often baffled by the constant realignment of their forces.

Equally common to all was the peculiar incompetence so often found among this quick-witted, seemingly intelligent, people. It was the kind of thing that, in the ordinary way, caused foreigners to smile and murmur, oh how Irish! They would go to the wrong house and shoot the wrong man. They would construct an elaborate bomb and forget some vital part. They would issue grandiloquent bulletins of phantom victories. Their courtiers would go abroad to pick up a load of rifles and, through some muddle, return with a consignment of margarine. It was all in the Irish tradition of knockabout farce, but, in the context of terror, made their deeds appear all the more grisly.

Their reasoning also followed a mysterious pattern of its own, beyond the powers of a non-Irish mind to grasp. To this, the Prog communiqué was no exception. The kidnapping, it revealed, was an act of revenge for the deaths of James Phee and Malachy Byrne, martyrs for Ireland: in other words, for the two young men who had inadvertently blown themselves up a few days previously. How were they martyrs? Who was to blame? And what had a mishap in Dublin to do with potty old Carrageen here in the west? Why had they picked on him? How had they ever heard of him?

'It's plumb crazy,' Marigold said, when the bulletin was over and the programme of Irish jigs resumed. Not even the coloured people at home could vie with this.

'Yes,' said Francis grimly, 'but they are bad as well as mad.

114

It only sounds like comic opera. In fact, it is Grand Guignol. They'll demand the release of some thug or other impossible thing, and kill the old chap in cold blood if they don't get it. Darling, you go on to bed. I'm going to fasten the outside doors and get a gun. Take Juno up with you.'

The whole affair, he reflected as he moved about his operations, might be entirely different from what it seemed. It could well be an act of private vengeance, for example. Something perhaps to do with that girl in the car – although, again, she might have been a decoy – or with one of Carrageen's lawsuits – although hardly that, as he invariably lost them. Anyone could ring Radio Eireann up and, describing himself as a Prog, give out a message like that, to put people off the scent or simply by way of a joke. Carrageen had no interest in politics, or in anything much except women and litigation. He had served in the war, of course, thus qualifying as a tool of British imperialism; but that was a long time ago, even for Ireland, and almost every Irishman of his class had done the same. And yet there had been other kidnappings every bit as stupid and pointless. The one thing you could be sure of was, there were people round here who knew all about it and would never breathe a word. As he had remarked to Marigold once – how he wished he never had brought her here! – you couldn't walk down the road but the countryside knew it.

'Well, that's that,' he said, entering Spion Kop with a shotgun over his arm, his face pale and set. 'I little thought, a couple of hours ago, that I should ever be missing Maguire.'

'What shall you do this morning?' he asked her, almost the minute she woke. 'I must go to church. Stay here if you like, but I'll have to lock you in and you mustn't open to anyone, not even the Guards.' Least of all the Guards, he nearly added. 'And don't on any account answer the telephone, either.'

'O.K. But don't feel so badly about it, Francis. This kind of thing is going on all over the world.'

In spite of himself, Francis could not keep back a chuckle. 'Trust you to look on the bright side!'

It was a bewildered, frightened set of people that collected at St Andrew's, this day of all the saints. Throughout the week they had been looking forward to the Battle of the Lessons, some betting on the Colonel, others on Maguire. Tension had increased by a regrouping of the factions that was almost worthy of the guerilla movement itself. Some viper had whispered to Miss Hackle that Maguire would give her a new harmonium, if she approached him in the right sort of way, and she had defected from the Colonel's camp forthwith. But this meant the loss to Maguire of Lady FitzBarlow, who went in for being liberal and up-to-the-minute but in no circumstances ever could side with Miss Hackle. Her ladyship brought with her various satellites of lower degree, so greatly disgusting the wives of the Colonel and the Rector, their nerves already strained by forced agreement, that both declared themselves neutral.

Then the terrible news came on the Saturday evening; and in the twingling of an eye, as at the outbreak of a war, all differences of opinion and clashes of temperament were forgotten.

'Welcome, my dear boy, welcome,' the Rector murmured, leaving the vestry on purpose to greet Francis as he took his place in the family pew. 'It was so like you to come. Maguire remains at the Castle?'

Francis explained that Maguire had put forward his projected trip to London by a day or two. 'Is anything known beyond what the wireless said?'

'Nothing. We are all completely in the dark. Some of the men are to meet in the vestry after Divine Service. Do not fail to join us there.' And the Rector wearily retired, to robe, collect up the choir and shepherd it into place.

He would not, he said when the time came to enter the pulpit, preach a sermon that day. There was but one thought in the minds of them all. And he need not ask their prayers for their abducted fellow parishioner, because those were assured. But he would ask them also to pray for the sadly misguided men who were guilty of this act. It was not easy, at such a moment, to exercise charity; but it was at such a moment that charity was the most urgently called for and of the greatest worth.

A long rumble broke from the Colonel here, like a roll of thunder in the Alps.

116

There was one more word, the Rector hurriedly continued, that he would say on this subject of Christian feeling. Their friend and fellow worshipper had his little ways and weaknesses – as who had not? – one of which was to make himself out as more of a black sheep than was really the case. Once again he had been hinting, as so often before, of some intended lapse which would remove him from among them, and giving rise to comment not always of the kindliest nature. Now, in this dreadful and unlooked-for way, he had been so removed. Some perhaps, listening now, might be inclined to reproach themselves for previous thought or words but he, their Rector, would urge them not to do so. Rather, he begged them put away all unkindness and uncharitableness towards this, or any, neighbour, extending to all the love and understanding of which all stood in equal need.

There was another growl from Colonel Beaulieu, sounding curiously like the words, 'silly old softy.'

To some of the congregation, however, the Rector's words came home. The elderly Lotharic had indeed, with many a wink and leer, let it be known that he would shortly be off on another amorous fugue. They had made cruel fun of it, as usual, and the blow which had fallen seemed a judgement more on themselves than on him. He was, all said and done, deserving of pity rather than blame or derision: a widower before he was thirty, his only son a wash-out (R.C. and a monk), poor, lonely, friendless, with little of joy behind him and none ahead. In their new-found solidarity, born of fear, his faults became irrelevant: he was one of them and because of that, for no other reason, victim of the Prog's inhuman and mindless rancour.

After the service the men all went to the vestry, as the Colonel had proposed and the Rector had agreed. But soon a difference in their purposes became apparent, causing the latter a new distress. His mind was on prayer, services of intercession, appeals to the guilty for a change of heart and to the public for whatever support they could give. The Colonel wanted action, the tougher the better. He had merely thought of the vestry as a means of fooling the local Progs – 'depend

117

upon it, the place is full of 'em' – into the belief that they were discussing parish affairs.

'We must smoke these fellows out and treat 'em like the rats they are,' he fumed, while the Rector dismally shook his head.

But where in the world should they begin? Nothing whatever was known, except that Carrageen had disappeared and his car was gone. Immediately after the wireless announcement, the Guards had rushed to the house and found what they took to be signs of homeric struggle; but this turned out, on deeper inquiry, to be its normal condition.

'I can't understand it,' said Dr McLeod. 'Why him? Ransom? He is not exactly rolling. And if they want money, as a rule they rob a bank.'

'Oh, he's a symbol or something,' FitzBarlow said impatiently. 'It's their Vengeance on Society, or some old tripe.'

'Well, "Society" is in a pretty bad way without them, though I shouldn't talk of it,' the doctor said. 'I've asked Radio Eireann to give out the drug he needs – for what good it may do.'

A silence fell on them all after that.

'Which of us saw him last?' asked the Colonel presently. 'I haven't run across him for days. Thought he had gone to earth.'

Most of the others were under the same impression.

'I passed him on the Limerick road on Monday,' Francis said. 'He seemed all right then. Had a girl in the car, a real one. Then after a bit a fellow came by and stopped me to ask if I'd seen them, and which way they went.'

'Do you think there's any connection?'

'Who can say what connects with what over here? This happened on Monday, and Fishy was only taken last night.'

'According to your man on the radio,' said Dr McLeod darkly.

'Well, the postman calls there, I imagine, and some old woman goes up to clean, and Quirke must be popping in and out all the time. You'd think the news would spread, if he'd been missing before.'

'Unless they were all involved,' growled the Colonel.

'I think you should tell the Guards,' the doctor persisted.

118

'You never know where a scrap of information may lead.'

No, Francis thought, indeed you did not. He remembered a 'scrap of information' brought to his notice once in a fashionable Dublin bar. Among the smartly dressed clientele a fellow in a dirty waterproof stood out, flanked by two henchmen, ordering drinks for which he did not pay. 'Know who that is?' Francis's companion murmured, and named one of the men most wanted in the North. 'Why doesn't someone call the Guards?' Francis murmured back, and got the laughing reply, 'Well now, I wonder!'

'Let's wait a little,' he said. 'It's rather a job to get the Guards on Sunday, what with drunken driving and football. And I'm inclined to think your man on the radio will pipe up again very soon and let us know what he's at.'

'Let us hope and pray we shall hear, at least, that Lord Carrageen is alive and well,' the Rector quavered.

'If we hear he's well, it's a lie,' the uncompromising McLeod retorted. 'And so could the rest of it be.'

On this depressing note the meeting dispersed, making only some practical arrangements for keeping in touch, the use of the telephone being deemed inadvisable.

'Walking today, are you?' the Colonel inquired of Francis. 'New car ditched already?'

Francis explained that the car in question belonged to Maguire, who had gone off to England in it, and that his own was in Paris.

'I'll give you a lift, then. Paris!' he grumbled, as they drove away. 'Julia and I had our honeymoon there, and there was nothing whatever to do. Never saw such a dreary place. We had a couple of rides in the Bois de Boulogne, otherwise sat and twiddled our thumbs. What on earth took you to Paris?'

'I wanted to see a bit of life,' Francis said, much diverted by his godfather's view of the *Ville Lumière*.

'Yes, very well, but you're married now,' the Colonel reproved him. His concept of life also differed from that of Francis. 'So Maguire's off to England? Pity. I'd have liked him here at the present time.'

'I thought there was some little disagreement?'

'Certainly not. You mean, the Lessons? Women's chatter.

119

When it came to the point, Maguire would have done as I told him.'

'Well, he was rather taking the bit between his teeth, apparently. Remember the Hunt?'

'And a jolly good day that was,' the Colonel responded, his face lighting up. 'Maguire was out of his depth, that's all. What your poor father could have – well, never mind. I've seen things of that sort before, in the Army. In the war they'd take a first-class NCO and commission him, because we were fighting for democracy. *I* wasn't, let me tell you, I was fighting the Hun. Well, the NCO never knew if he was on his head or his heels after that, and it was all a great cock-up. Now you take that Hunt, Maguire dressed up like an organ grinder's monkey and trying to come it. When we were drawing near Rougemain, I just said to him, Fall back, Maguire, there's a good chap, we've a job to do forward. And he said, Very good, sir, and fell back at once. I tell you, *Maguire is all right*. Mad as a Hatter, but perfectly sound. And we could do with him now.'

When they reached the Castle, the Colonel smiled his approval as Francis produced his massive key to the front door. He only wished the others were half as security-minded. No, he would not come in for a drink, he was off on a quiet little recce, but he sent his love to Marigold.

'What on earth can she make of all this?' he wanted to know.

'Says it's just like anywhere else in the world.'

The Colonel made the trumpeting noise which, with him, indicated amusement. 'That young lady has pluck. Well, now, Francis, keep your ear to the ground and your eyes peeled. There may be some round here who'd be ready to drop a hint without actually saying a word, y'know how they are.'

'I never can understand how they got their name for courage.'

'Oh, they can be brave enough, VCs, fasting to death and all that, but only if people are looking on. Perfect swank casteth out fear, as the good book says. Now, mind what I told you, keep awake, and we'll meet tomorrow.'

The simplicities and certainties of the gallant Colonel had done much to restore and refresh young Barraclough's mind.

That evening, his prediction about 'your man on the radio'

came true. They had left the wireless on all afternoon, patiently enduring the Sunday round of football commentary, spiritual advice, new Irish poems, so oddly like the old, and gramophone records requested by hospital patients, in case a programme should be interrupted for a special announcement. By the time the Angelus rang at six, their minds were fairly numb with boredom; but immediately afterwards they were rewarded by a further bulletin from the Progressives concerning the captured lord. Their terms were, as Francis had also predicted, the release of two notorious thugs, one of whom had set fire to a crowded dance-hall and the other, rained explosives from a helicopter on to a private house, in the belief that it was the British Embassy. These conditions were to be met within forty-eight hours or the prisoner would be executed.

'Do you think they really mean it?' Marigold asked, her eyes wide.

'Yes.'

But did they? The authorities refused the demand or to negotiate in any way with the Progs. The time limit expired, and for a day no more was heard: then came a second message, allowing another forty-eight hours. This too was ignored, and again the period of grace was extended. Was it a question of life or death, or was it simple foolery? Now it seemed one, now the other: the only sure thing about it was, that no one could be sure.

# Chapter Sixteen

The Government refusal and the Prog's repeated extensions, however, still lay ahead on Monday morning, when Francis saddled a horse and rode to the barracks in Ballinaween. That the girl in Carrageen's car had something to do with his disappearance was possible, because, in Ireland, anything was possible; but it was not at all likely, and Francis assumed the Sergeant would make short work of it. In the event, the outcome amazed even him, a result he would have sworn was beyond the power of any compatriot to produce.

The officer in question was a miserable man this day. He had never heard of Talleyrand or his famous dictum, that zeal was to be avoided; but he had faithfully observed the principle throughout his professional life. He was, from the bottom of his heart, a man of peace. The arrest of Maguire was the first he had made in sixteen years, and the consequence of that had proved the value of inactivity. Now all his tranquil comfort was ended. Superiors in the Force, members of the Special Branch, were on their way, would soon arrive, expecting to hear that some line of inquiry was already being pursued. But such was not the case. There was nothing, absolutely nothing, to report, nothing to go on, no clue, no information. He had not even found a contemporary photo to publish, although there were dozens of the fellow taken in his handsome youth. The woman who worked in Carrageen's house had been in hospital all that week. It was not even sure that his lordship was seized on the Saturday, as he lived some way from the village and never was much in the public eye. Various people had noted his car on the Monday because he had got a real live girl with him at last, but none could remember when or how often they saw it since.

The Sergeant listened wearily as Francis began the familiar recital, with the added detail of his lordship stopping and introducing his friend as Rose O'Malley; but as it went on, he suddenly pricked up his ears.

'You are saying, then, how a lad you didn't know came after Lord Carrageen and stopped as well, asking did you see him and which way did he go?' he inquired, eyeing the informant closely.

'That's it.'

'And what did this fellow look like, at all?'

'Oh, just ordinary. A countryman, middle-aged, a bit warm, might have been drinking. Had a very loud voice.'

'What class of a car was he in?'

'One of those old black Morris Minors they have.'

The Sergeant slowly and carefully wrote this down, as if it had been a confession of murder.

'Why didn't you tell us before, Mr Francis?' he asked then.

'Before what? before the kidnapping? How could I know there would be one?'

'Before today, before this. The radio message was on Saturday night.'

'It didn't seem of any importance.'

'Did it not?' The Sergeant gravely wrote down something more. 'And why does it seem important now?' he resumed, looking up.

'It doesn't. I mentioned it to Dr McLeod, and he advised me to tell you.'

The Sergeant recorded this, and went on: 'Then, but for Dr McLeod, you'd have said nothing?'

'Probably not.'

The Sergeant stared at the notes he had taken, his forehead puckered in thought. He was engaged in a characteristic Irish practice which may have sprung from centuries of story-telling impromptu beside the fire: he was fitting this new little piece into the hazy picture he had already with more regard to dramatic effect than to logic or commonsense. No one else had mentioned the countryman in a Morris Minor. No one else in fact had seen him, Francis having diverted him to the Mallow Road. But Francis had clean forgotten this, and the Sergeant could hardly divine it: he was, therefore, toying with the idea that the countryman had never existed at all and that

Francis had invented him for a sinister reason of his own.

'What car were you driving yourself, Mr Francis?' he began again, with a powerful sense of making headway at last.

'Maguire had lent me his Marina.'

'He'll corroborate that, I daresay?'

'Really, Sergeant . . . ! He would, of course, if he were here, but he's gone to England.'

That much, his interlocutor knew. Miss Hackle, her mind fixed on the new harmonium, had blown in earlier that morning to say how strange it was, they had all expected Mr Maguire at church the day before, but he never came, young Barraclough was there instead, for once in his life, and told them of Mr Maguire's sudden departure, he was to have gone the following week, had invited people to shoot on Monday, there might be nothing in it, but it did seem odd, and in view of this dreadful affair she thought it as well to report it. She had rambled on and on, repeating herself without any sign of fatigue, while the Sergeant grew more and more exasperated; but now . . .

He communed with himself earnestly for a period, and then produced a bombshell. 'I'm thinking, Mr Francis, there's no offence intended, now, but I'm thinking, it might be helpful if you surrendered your passport.'

'Surrender my passport!' cried Francis, aghast. 'Whatever for?'

'To oblige me, Mr Francis,' the Sergeant pleaded. 'On a voluntary basis!'

Then no one, he reflected, could reproach him for taking no steps whatever.

'Most certainly I will not. I shall need it myself. I've been trying to get off to France since I don't know when.'

'Well now, if you were in the want of it, I could let you have it back,' the Sergeant proposed.

The tides of lunacy were rising yet again: one fine day, the young man thought, they would engulf him for ever. 'Then what would be the point of your taking it?' he demanded, in something like awe.

'A routine precaution,' the Sergeant replied, with solemnity.

'But you don't seriously imagine I'm involved in this matter?'

'I suspect everybody, until the contrary is proved,' was the candid reply.

'Then you had better collect everyone's passport. No, I'm sorry, there is nothing doing. I never heard such nonsense in my life.' Here Shreddie the horse poked his head through the door and whinnied loudly, as if in agreement. 'I can't keep that animal standing about, I'm off. Good morning.' And he rode away, leaving the arm of the law to its own devices.

Old ways die hard in the west of Ireland and, apart from his philosophy of live and let live, the Sergeant had an archaic respect for the likes of young Barraclough. He frowned and shook his head at the abrupt and lordly manner, but in his bones he felt it was fitting. Soon afterwards, however, the men of a different mould began to appear, the hard men from Dublin, smart, efficient, equipped with radio cars, helicopters, walkie-talkies and every blessed gadget you could think of. They had no need to worry about procedure, because they did not live here; and they set to work at once, taking aerial pictures of the country, combing it yard by yard, setting up road-blocks and observation-points and, in general, carrying on in a way that Talleyrand would have deplored.

The trouble was that, for all their zeal, they finished up hardly a penny the wiser than the Sergeant himself, while causing no end of commotion. As they knew none of the local people by sight, they stopped all who came past the road-blocks and badgered them without mercy. Into their net swam the rural Dean, on his way to visit the Rector, which annoyed the Protestants: Dr Clancy, speeding to the confinement of Mrs Denis Halloran, the schoolmaster's wife, which led to high words and threats of official complaint: the butcher from Ballinaduff on delivery rounds, who threw open the doors of his van and sardonically invited them to search for his lordship's carcase there; a pair of Jehovah's Witnesses, who harangued them on the state of the world until their heads fairly spun; and a crowd of others, engaged in equally harmless or useful errands.

The only helpful witness they found wasted more of their

125

time than anyone else. Looshie Quirke made no secret of his opinion that Mr Francis Barraclough knew a great deal more about the case than he should. He had no reason to love Carrageen, who went driving about with his wife and had smashed up his valuable car. Furthermore, Mr Patrick Kevin Maguire, the rightful owner of the Castle, Francis having been disinherited by his father for disgraceful conduct, had likewise suddenly disappeared. Maguire was a client of his and they had an appointment for this very day, to discuss matters of ownership disputed by Barraclough, still living at the Castle on suffrance: yet, without a word to him, Maguire had allegedly run to England on the night of Lord Carrageen's capture, whereas he was to have gone there tomorrow at earliest, for a regimental reunion at the end of the week. The message supposed to come from the Progs might well be a hoax. If he, Quirke, were in charge of this inquiry, he would follow the Barraclough line up before anything else.

Some of this farrago had already come to the Gardai's ears, and the Sergeant had also informed them of the stranger's pursuit of Lord Carrageen's car, as related by Francis. An immense all-out effort now was launched to find him, should he exist, the girl Rose O'Malley and the present address of Maguire. For the latter they applied to the British Embassy in Dublin, whose military attaché contacted the War Office, which made inquiries and signalled back that as regards the reunion nothing was known, but that of Maguire's address on the pension list was Castle Reef, Ballinaween. Twelve Rose O'Malleys were traced and all but one, who was on spiritual Retreat in Cork, were safely at home. An even more intensive search produced the man in the Morris Minor, who had no connection with any girl of that name. Weaving about the road, Lord Carrageen's car had bumped into his, drawn up by Kavanagh's Lounge, just as he, Michael Kenny, was coming out. His lordship never troubled to stop and Kenny, who had a few jars taken, raced after him to demand an apology and the price of a few jars more.

Reluctantly, the Gardai closed the Barraclough file.

The taking of aerial pictures had also fanned the fires of local discontent. When the helicopter first appeared over the

126

village, many leaped to the conclusion that it belonged to the Progs and that they were about to be bombed in reprisal for something or other. All the advice they had ever received on war-time emergencies was contained in a single leaflet which, being in Irish, nobody understood and which in any case dealt with global nuclear warfare. People indoors rushed out, and those outside flew into the nearest building. The Guards had to drive round and round, bawling for calm through loud-speakers, and were shouted and jeered at as they passed. The animals were equally unnerved by the strange new creature overhead, and there was no way in which to reassure them. The cattle raced wildly about as if attacked by a swarm of bees, sheep sprang over their hedges and poured down the lanes, the dogs barked furiously all together, and Miss Hilary Baggot, thrown by a startled horse, broke a leg.

The Gardai had so much work to do, reporting on these occurrences, that the duty for which they had come was gravely impeded.

Then journalists began to arrive, first from the local, next from the Dublin, and lastly from even the English, press. Several of the Irishmen had been here before, when what promised to make a beautiful story, 'Famous Castle Bequeathed to Butler', originally broke; but they had been sadly disappointed. Francis held the view that private affairs were private, and Maguire looked on newspapermen as showers. Neither would say a word, and the reporters were obliged to fall back on such gossip, comment or pure invention as they could wheedle out of the other inhabitants. They thus returned to base each with a different tale, the one common factor being libel so obvious that no rational editor could print it.

They had been mortified by the experience and looked on their new assignment as a chance to make good all round. Barraclough might insist that his father's will was no concern of theirs, but the kidnapping of an Anglo-Irish peer was another kettle of fish. It was a matter of public interest and international importance, and if he had any decency at all he would help them as much as he could. Then, once the contact was made and entry to the Castle established, they would use their charm, address and powers of persuasion to winkle the facts of the legacy from him too.

It soon turned out that Francis lacked even the modicum of decency required for their success. If they telephoned, he cut them off with a polite but firm 'good day'. If they banged on the door, it was not opened, and when they made to push in they found it locked. They nosed about, trying the other entrances one by one with the same result; they attempted to prise up a window or two, but these were fastened as well.

The house appeared to be either deserted or in a state of siege. It was very strange, for they had been assured that both Francis and his wife were there. And presently something occurred that was stranger still. A few of the more fanatical spirits hid themselves in the bushes, to keep watch until a sign of life should come from within. An hour passed and the rain drove down, soaking them to the skin, but faithfully they held to their purpose.

Then, 'Look what's coming!' muttered one with horrid glee. 'The Innocent Abroad!'

A young English colleague, whom they had written off as a fool, walked out from under the avenue trees and made for the door, on which he gently knocked. The spies in the rhododendrons fairly hugged themselves, to see this empty hope. But, to their surprise and indignation, the door was opened almost immediately: Francis appeared, his face lit up, and they heard him exclaim, 'Reresby, dear man, what brings you here? Come in at once and get those wet things off.' And Reresby Marvell went inside, the door swung to and the key turned audibly in the lock. The watching men could hardly believe their eyes and ears. There was no question of an agreed signal between confederates, for Francis clearly had not expected the visit. There was something well nigh supernatural about it, and quite beyond their powers of understanding.

The explanation was simplicity itself, and would have enraged them had they known it. Juno was on guard in the hall. As soon as she heard their noisy plebeian bangs, she 'placed' them as undesirable and uttered her warning growl. Marvell's modest tap qualified him for admission, and she hurried to fetch the master, wagging her tail and smiling in cosy approval.

'How long ago Oxford does seem,' Francis said, when

Reresby was comfortably seated by the fire with a drink in his hand. 'Did you know I'm an old married man? My wife will be in presently, one of the foxhounds has whelped and she's drooling over the puppies. What are you doing these days?'

'I'd better make a clean breast of it,' Reresby said, after suitable congratulations on the marriage. 'I'm here for the *Daily Chronicle* – getting nowhere, I may say – and I thought I'd look you up. But don't think I want to be a bore.'

'A newshawk? You? Bless us! There's no question of boring. I'd help if I could, but I know damn-all,' Francis said, heaving a sigh. 'Just that the poor old boy was dragged off by some yobs, that he has angina, and may well die of that if the yobs don't kill him first.'

'It's a horrible business, and I'm desperately sorry,' Reresby said. 'But truly, I didn't come here to pump you. I've wired the paper already that I'm wasting time and money. On the form, Carrageen is probably tied up in a council house near Dublin, with all the neighbours in the know. I'm expecting new instructions, and wanted to see you before I left.'

'Well, you must stay to luncheon anyhow. I shouldn't have asked you a week ago, when my wife was cook, but now we can do you like a prince.'

Maguire was hardly gone when Mrs Jeffars had reappeared, unbidden, and taken over. With her came a new assortment c troglodytes, who were put to work cleaning the place, much neglected of recent times, and removing the barriers erected by Maguire. In her leisure moments Mrs Jeffars went on safari herself, listing his other misdemeanours, among them that he had – just like his impudence – 'borrowed' the Major's best leather suitcase. All attempts to reason with her came to nothing and, what with the worry of the missing man and the pleasure of eating well again, Francis soon gave them up.

The two friends sat, agreeably drinking and talking together. Reresby regaled his host with an account of the Gardai's endeavours of which, pent up by the pressmen, Francis had not even heard. In spite of the dreadful circumstances, he could not help laughing from time to time, nor could Reresby when, in his turn, Francis described his interview with the Sergeant.

'What a wonderful story it would make,' he said wistfully. 'How funny it all would be, if it weren't so frightful.'

'That could be Ireland's epitaph.'

Now a van pulled up outside and Juno burst into frenzied barking.

'The postman,' Francis said, getting up. 'He's extremely late, I thought he wasn't coming. I'll have to leave you for a minute, he refuses to get out of his van.'

It was quite a few minutes before he returned, bringing some letters and helplessly laughing again.

'Held up in one of the roadblocks!' he said. 'He won't wear his uniform, thinking it puts the dogs against him. So the Guards imagined they really were on to something at last, stolen mailcar, redoubtable character ... It's as good as a play, better than most. Mind if I glance through these?'

'A rude postcard from one of my rude French friends,' he commented frowning. 'They keep on at me, to know when I'm coming back.' And he made to throw it on the fire.

'You might let me see,' said Reresby, snatching it. 'Hm, yes. Very poor taste.'

The picture was of a pretty girl, naked but for a skirt of real feathers which, when blown up, fluttered up to reveal her intimate parts, sketched with notable realism: the caption read, 'M'as tu vraiment vue?'

'Nice friends you have,' Reresby chuckled, blowing away with keen enjoyment. 'May I look at the other side?'

'By all means, if it amuses you.'

'It's in English,' Reresby informed him, 'and very colloquial. "Lovely weather here, though I don't get out much, too busy, ha ha! Never thought a colleen could be such hot stuff. Must be the flaming mop of hair. Hoping this finds you, as it leaves me, dans la vie en Rose!!!" From someone called "Fishy".'

'What' shouted Francis. 'Here, give me that!'

'All right, manners, manners.'

'Oh no! Oh no!' said Francis weakly, after running hastily through it. 'It is. From Fishy. His writing. His style. It's your **man**! Carrageen, the one they are scouring the country for.' And he threw himself back in his chair, shaken by wild laughter in which Reresby joined.

130

'And you were for putting it on the fire!'

Francis nodded, unable to speak.

'Then after all, Ireland is just funny, full-stop,' said Reresby, recovering a little. 'But what does it all mean? The radio messages and so on?'

'Anyone's guess. Mine is, nothing. Oh, what a blessed relief! Reresby, you'll excuse me, I have to pass this on at once. Sit here, look after yourself, and Mrs Jeffars will give you lunch if I'm not back on time.'

He was on his way to the door when Reresby stopped him. 'Francis,' he said, on a note of appeal, 'you couldn't hold this back for a while? It's such a marvellous scoop for me. I don't mind telling you, frankly, the paper thinks I'm not so hot. They'll change their tune when this comes over.'

'My dear fellow . . .' Francis began hesitantly, moved by the anguished entreaty in Reresby's eyes. 'It's not the press or the Guards I'm going to. There are men here, friends of that naughty old wretch, who have been worried sick about him. I can't leave them in the dark, indeed I cannot. But I'll swear them to secrecy, they can be trusted.'

'Nobody could be trusted with a gem like this,' Reresby pleaded. Newspapers had taught him that much. 'What a story, with all the background, police, helicopters, postman arrested . . . Francis, be a sport! I need my job, and I think I'm about to lose it.'

'But look here, old chap. Today is Saturday, tomorrow is Sunday, Remembrance Sunday. We are all to meet after church and talk things over. Your piece can't appear until Monday now. Am I to sit with those men and hear them groaning, when a word from me would clear it all up?'

'I know it's a lot to ask,' Reresby sadly agreed. 'Too much, perhaps.' But he was looking at Francis with the same piteous appeal as before.

'I'll do it,' said Francis slowly. 'I'm a hound and they'll never forgive me, but I will. But how do you get the story out of the country? The telephone hath ears to hear.'

'Oh, that,' said the other joyously. 'I'll write the piece, here if I may, and scramble it all into cable-ese. The telephone will

131

get nothing but earache. Francis, you're the whitest man on earth.'

'I'm a stinkeroo,' said Francis grimly. 'But I'm going to tell Marigold, whatever you say. She has been eating her heart out. I'll lock her up until Monday, if you insist, but hear this, she shall.'

He set off at once on this mission, pausing only to inform Mrs Jeffars that there was a guest for lunch. The kitchen reeked deliciously of hare a-jugging, but the cook's face was sour and set.

'And we'll have a bottle of the Talbot, if you please.'

'If it isn't all drunk,' quoth Mrs Jeffars. 'Mr Francis, did you know there was min in the bushes, be the top of the drive? And up to no good, I'm thinking.' For nothing escaped her.

'No, really? I'll attend to them. But I want a word with the mistress first.' He was halfway to the kennels before he realized that he had both referred to Marigold as 'the mistress' and ordered a bottle of the master's wine.

Coward, is it? thought Mrs Jeffars, and her features relaxed in a motherly smile.

Marigold was cradling one of the puppies in her arms, while the mother danced anxiously round on her hind legs.

'Marigold, Fishy is safe! He's in Paris, with his fruit, the carroty-poll we saw. I've just had a card from him. And I've got an old Oxford friend, awfully nice chap, with us for lunch. So put that revolting quadruped down and prink yourself up.'

'Fishy, safe? Oh Francis!' In her emotion she rained kisses down on the pup till the dam yelped in agony. 'Take him then,' she said, putting him back in his basket. 'You'd think I was a Prog myself,' she complained, as the hound feverishly licked her offspring over, testing for injuries. 'Fishy in Paris! Doesn't he know of the hue and cry?'

'Why should he? Anyhow, the card was posted on Monday. Hurry up, there's a dear, we'll talk about it later. Go in the back way and unlock the front door. I have a small little job on hand. Come, Juno!'

Juno lost no time in flushing the bedraggled pressmen out of their observation post and herding them off her land.

'Isn't it great, Mrs Jeffars, did you hear, Fishy is safe?'

Marigold called as she ran by the kitchen.

'Thanks be to God, ma'am!' Luckily for Mr Marvell, she had no idea in the world who Fishy might be.

'My wife is just coming,' Francis said, returning to his visitor. 'I hope you will like her. A homely girl and none too bright, but with an agreeable disposition.'

Reresby smiled. 'Francis, would she allow me to do my piece here? and come back tomorrow, to send it? There's nobody in the London office today. I'd feel safer. It would be awful if the others got wind of it somehow, and they boggle at nothing.'

'I believe you. Juno has just seen a part of them off. But why come back? Stay overnight and telephone in the morning when everyone is at church. I don't envy you, the switchboard stopgap is all but moronic. In fact, you could probably send the piece *en clair* without exciting suspicion. Do stay! we'd love to have you.'

'It would be a help indeed, many thanks,' Reresby said. 'And one thing more – could I possibly keep the card and send it over as proof?'

'Of course, but it won't be there until Wednesday or Thursday.'

'No, but I can tell them it's coming.'

'Jokes about the moron aside, will you have to mention Carrageen by name?'

'Dear me, no. The news editor fixed all that, code words for everyone, police, Special Branch, the lot. He said, take no chances and rely on nothing.'

'He seems to know Ireland.'

'He is Irish himself.'

Now Marigold came in, her usual county attire of jeans, woollies and Wellingtons hurriedly exchanged for a little French dress and, radiant with happiness, more bewitching than ever. 'You're very welcome,' she said to Reresby, giving him her hand at once. 'And you've come at the right moment. We've had wonderful news and we'll need to celebrate.'

The gong boomed out, as if to say, Come on and begin.

'He knows,' Francis said. 'This is Reresby Marvell from the *Daily Chronicle* and he's going to write the story here and

133

send it tomorrow. And all those yahoos out there will be as sick as Kilkenny cats.'

As they went to the dining-room, Marigold leading the way, Reresby murmured to Francis, 'Very homely indeed, you poor chap. You should have prepared me better.'

'What I can't understand,' Marigold began, as Mrs Jeffars took the meal from the hatch and placed it on the sideboard, 'is why old Fishy . . .'

'*Tout à l'heure,*' said Francis hurriedly.

'*Et pourquoi?*'

'*Parceque je te dis.* Not a word to a soul until Monday, *ma chère,*' he resumed when Mrs Jeffars had gone. 'Reresby is to hog all the glory himself.'

'Why, I did sing out to her in passing that Fishy was safe, and she thanked God for it,' Marigold said, helping herself to hare. 'But she sounded kind of vague. Most likely her mind was on lunch.'

'Well, she'll have to be held incommunicado just in case. A bit of luck that she dreads the telephone. What were you going to say?'

'Only, it seems odd of Fishy to write just to you.'

'For all we know, he's written to others.'

'Don't be so dumb, Francis! They'd have come running up here in two shakes of a lambs tail, to put your mind at rest.'

'Then perhaps he wanted to make you jealous,' he said, flushing up, and avoiding Reresby's eye.

'Maybe,' his wife agreed with a chuckle. 'His lordship had a go at me,' she explained to the guest. 'Red currant jelly? My, this is good. Now here's a funny thing. Cooking is supposed to be an art. Well, with the other arts, writing, painting, people can never be sure if their work is any good or not. But with cookery, there's no mistake.' She heaved a gentle sigh.

Much as they relished the proofs of Mrs Jeffars skill, they did not linger over them as Reresby was pining to start his work; and when, later on, he read out what he had written the other two declared that it was masterly. That his superior in London had doubts of his ability was not altogether surprising. At Oxford he had read Classics and, in his tutor's eyes, done himself much credit; but it had not fitted him for everyday

134

work on a paper. He lacked what editors call a news sense, that is, he never could spot the headline behind some trivial piece of tomfoolery. But, given material such as he had now, he could present it lucidly and attractively, and did so with a grave respect that made it sound all the wilder and more extravagant. It grieved the artist in him that the limitations of the *genre* forced him to begin with Lord Carrageen's whereabouts, instead of whipping them out with a bang as the coda; but his account of the whole affair, the measures taken by the police and their results, the devoted work of his colleagues – to which he paid handsome tribute – was journalism at its best.

'A pity you had to leave Rosie out,' Francis gurgled, when he was done.

'No, no, better as it is. Let the reader imagine him visiting the Louvre or the Sacré Coeur. Farmyard stuff would only spoil it.'

'I can hardly wait for Monday,' Francis confessed, wishing however that Sunday did not come in between.

Then they passed the merriest of evenings together and went late to bed in the highest of good humours.

# Chapter Seventeen

But Marigold and Reresby were blithe, alien and free. Francis had invisible irons on his leg. As he took his place in church next morning, the tokens of his caste all round him, tattered flags, memorial urns and tablets with their elegant inscriptions, his heart began to sink. Today the Rector made no reference to the abduction, but spoke briefly of what they were to remember, paid tribute to the gallant soldier who could not be with them again and gave thanks to God for the son who should carry the old name on. And hearing this, the son could have wished himself at the bottom of the sea.

His heart sank again as the few of them assembled in the vestry afterwards; but the meeting did not go at all as he had feared. Their number was swelled today by Captain Barrie, the Hunt Secretary, who had last appeared in Church for his wedding, many long years ago. It must have taken more than Remembrance Sunday to bring him here, thought Francis, and he was right. What followed was not so much a council of war as a service of commination. Even if the Rector sighed and wrung his hands from time to time, it was rather from force of habit than from any heartfelt protest. For the subject was the cowardly, treacherous, unspeakably caddish, behaviour of Lord Ballysprocket.

This individual was of a species not unknown among the former ascendency. To put it baldly, he had jumped, or done what he could to jump, on to the republican bandwaggon. His name frequently appeared at the foot of letters to newspapers, denouncing the partition of Ireland, the internment of terrorists in the North, the 'torture' that suspects allegedly suffered and the brutality of British troops towards the defenceless Catholic population; and, at one moment, he had dramatically renounced his British nationality and applied for an Irish passport.

Nevertheless, he hung on firmly to the title which his forbears had received from the British Crown and which still counted for much in his native land. This having of things both ways was typical of the species, and for that matter of the country at large. But now he had suddenly come out with a statement, splashed across all the Sunday papers, describing British titles as an anachronism, undemocratic and offensive to fellow citizens; he had also revealed that he was about to relinquish his, and called on his peers, if 'worthy of the name of Irishmen', to follow his example.

'What a time to choose!' growled Colonel Beaulieu.

'Yellow,' said FitzBarlow. 'But he always was. He thinks the Progs will nab him next. And I'm sure I hope they do.'

'Yes, yes, all that,' said the Colonel impatiently. 'But we need him in the Lords. The bloodsport cranks are off again, and if they get their way, it's going to spread over here. And with Fishy gone . . .' He relapsed into brooding silence. No one could say he was a callous man, but first things came first with him, and when hunting was in his mind there was not much room for anything else.

'Fat lot of use Ballysprocket would be.'

'Fair play for him, he's a hunting man. And we shall need every voice we can get.'

'I can't understand the Lords,' Dr McLeod said with a puzzled frown. 'Only the British can be peers of the realm. Why didn't they throw him out when he reneged.'

'Oh, you are thinking of us as an institution,' FitzBarlow said, with a short laugh. 'When you belong, it's a kind of club, with club jokes and club bores. Ballysprocket is both.'

'What do you say, young Francis?' asked Captain Barrie.

'I suppose, sir, he thinks our number is up. He's trying to adjust or integrate or whatever they call it.'

'Wants to have his cake and eat it, you mean! But the people here are sharp enough to rumble him. I should expect them to be disgusted.'

'I think they would rather admire him,' Francis replied. 'It is what they would do themselves.'

'Something in that,' the Captain conceded. 'Look at that hoary old villain McNally! Enlisted 1911, fought in World War One, came home and joined the IRA, then went back to

England to work. Now drawing three pensions, War Office, IRA and British Old Age.'

'The Viscount Bally and Mr McNally, are brothers under the skin,' smiled Francis.

The colonel cleared his throat. 'Any chance of pulling that young idiot out of his monk-hole?' he wondered. 'If he inherits, I mean?' He was referring to Carrageen's son and heir, the Honourable Tristram Battie, now Father Pius, OSD.

'None, I fear,' moaned the Rector. 'Highly improbable.'

The Colonel grunted.

'Has anyone heard from him, by the way?' asked Dr McLeod.

Nobody had.

'He isn't allowed to read the papers, or get in touch with the outside world,' Captain Barrie affirmed, with authority 'No, he's gone to the dogs, let him be. Bad as Ballysprocket himself.'

'One of the Ballysprockets married a Fahy,' FitzBarlow mused. 'But that was a hundred years ago.'

'Blood always comes out,' the Colonel growled. 'But what a time to do it!'

This brought the meeting back to the question of Carrageen and, since there was nothing to say that had not been said the week before, it joined in cursing the ineptitude of the Guards until it went its separate ways.

At home Francis found Marigold applying restoratives to Reresby, supine on a Chesterfield, pale and spent. In a curious way, he somehow looked older than at breakfast time.

'It was the telephone,' she explained.

'I never knew anything like it,' the invalid croaked, 'and I'm counting Morocco. First I waited half an hour with nothing happened at all, except for background noises that hardly seemed of this earth. Then at last I got through and a dim little faraway voice asked who it was. Give me the newsroom, I bawled: can you hear me? Plainly, it whispered, no need to shout. Then another voice broke in and said, Are ye holdin'? I said, I was talkin, and would it get off the line. But it kept breaking in every minute or so all the way through. Oh yes – I'm forgetting. At one stage we got cut off completely. I had to start all over again. God only knows what kind of galimatias they got at the other end. Probably they think I am mad.'

'Oh, that often happens, I should have warned you,' Francis encouraged him. 'You go up on one line and the fellow in London comes down on another. You got a good one, and he got a bad. He'll have heard you as if you were in the next room.'

'Do you mean that?' asked Reresby doubtfully. 'If my piece should miscarry . . .'

Here the telephone burst into cry and Francis hurried to answer it.

'Hold on for a London call,' said the adenoidal voice of the Sunday stopgap. Ten or fifteen minutes passed, full of the sounds that Reresby had noted. They were made by the stopgap's baby girl, crooning, burping and pulling plugs out at random, to suck with hearty relish.

Another, male, voice came on and boomed, 'Can you hear me?'

'Yes, very well. Please don't shout.'

'What that?'

'I hear you very well.'

'Is Reresby Marvell there?'

'Yes, but he's having a rest. Can I take a message?'

'What?'

'A MESSAGE?'

'Who are you? Do speak up.'

'My name is Barraclough. Marvell is staying with me,' Francis screamed.

'Oh. Tell him, the piece is first-rate. Have you got that?' There came another deafening, 'First-rate! Ask him to ring when he can.'

'Your piece is first-rate,' said Francis hoarsely, returning with a hand in his ear. 'And you are to ring when you can. Thank you, Marigold, I'll take the same.' He fell into a chair and closed his eyes. 'The simplest operation here is like a day's work anywhere else. And the Post Office has taken to stamping our letters, "Conserve Energy". What can it mean?'

'First-rate?' Reresby was babbling. 'Did he say, first-rate?'

'Yes, if my shattered eardrums didn't mislead me.'

139

'Come to my arms, my beamish boy! O frabjous day! Calooh! Callay! Thank you Francis, and thank you Marigold. To think, I was so down yesterday, I near as dammit gave you a miss! And near as dammit, you put that card on the fire!' Feeling himself again, Reresby sat up and took a pull at his glass.

'Can I see this famous card?' Marigold wished to know.

'Certainly not,' said Francis promptly. 'Yes, things have turned out well. When you are somewhat stronger, you will ring London again. After lunch, when the normal – if that is the word – staff have returned from their devotions.'

A great peace descended on them all. After recruiting his forces further with roast beef and apple-pie, Reresby nerved himself to telephone once more and was much delighted with the glowing if guarded praises he received. 'You *are* quite positive?' the newsroom asked once. 'Absolutely. Proof will be posted express tomorrow.' 'Good lad. Unless some world figure gets shot tonight, you're to lead the paper.'

Later that evening, Francis ran across Mrs Jeffars in her Sunday hat, preparing to leave the house.

'Where are you going, if I may ask?'

'Why, to the six-o'clock, sir,' she replied. 'I was too busy this morning what with the lunch.'

'Must you go?'

'Must I get Mass, Mr Francis? Indeed I must.'

'Those men in the bushes earlier on were all from newspapers. If they are back, they will probably try to get something out of you.'

'Well, then, I'll disappoint them!' And, with a toss of her head, she went her way.

Satisfied that the last little hole was stopped, Francis went back to the others. Now nothing remained but to relax and wait for developments.

# Chapter Eighteen

There were two hotels in Ballinaween, The Castle View and Murphy's, and whichever a person went to, he wished with all his heart he had gone to the other. In the summer they overflowed with tourists and the bars were open all night; but in winter they were more or less empty, with only the bar-trade to keep them alive.

At present they were doing well with the newspaper boys, who were out most of the day and spent freely in the lounge on their return. Both establishments had a sing-song on Sunday night – The Castle View called theirs a 'musical entertainment' – which continued till three or four o'clock on Monday morning. The boys, therefore, were disposed to lie in today, as breakfast never was served before ten, and their assignment had become about as demanding as a papal election.

From eight or so onward, the telephones in both places were shrieking their heads off, but no one replied, as the staff was resting too. It was after eleven when the boys came sleepily trickling down, to find the residue of their supper still on the dining room table. The national papers had been delivered, that is to say, the front door had been opened and the parcel thrown on the mat: the English would only arrive with the evening bus. The Irish boys saw their contributions cut to a very few lines when they were not omitted altogether. It was raining cats and dogs. Gloomily, the hungry men started games of poker to while the time away until the kitchen should stir.

Those in The Castle View were presently startled to see a car drive up and a Garda in officer's kit step from it. They threw down their cards and rushed at him, hoping he brought them a story. All he would say was, he wanted a word with the *Daily Chronicle* man, Mr Marvell; and, on hearing that Marvell had moved into Castle Reef, he shut his lips grimly as if he might have known it. He drove off again without another word and, sadly, the men went back to their game.

When the officer reached the Castle, Reresby was halfway to Limerick in the local taxi. Francis had deemed it unwise for

Fishy's card to be posted in Ballinaween or Ballinaduff, Radio Eireann having broadcast Reresby's despatch verbatim in the early news. All he was able to say was, that Marvell had gone out and would not be back for some hours.

'Is it that piece he wrote for the paper?' he inquired innocently. 'Journalists don't reveal their sources of information, you know.'

'Mebbe not. I'd like a word with yourself. May I come in?'

'Do, do.'

He took him to the library and they both sat down. The officer scrutinized him for some moments, sizing him up, this pleasant young man who looked him full in the eye as if he had nothing to fear. But, if the Gardai surmises were founded, he had a good deal to fear.

'There was a long call to London from your house yesterday morning,' he began. 'And a call back from London shortly after. Then another call to London in the afternoon.'

'That is so,' Francis confirmed. 'I must say, when the Gardai are right, they are right.' And he smiled, as if in relief that the case was in such competent hands.

His civil commendation cut the officer to the quick. The Gardai had made themselves so unloved that the neighbourhood was in ecstacies at their discomfiture. The entire nation, come to that, would be having the laugh of their lives. Now this young limb was daring to mock at him openly.

'You mentioned sources,' he said angrily. 'As we see it, there's only one. If you had knowledge that we had not, it was your duty to tell us. Wasting our time is a public mischief.'

'I, waste your time?' said Francis, who was primed for this attack. 'It seems to me, that some of you have been wasting your own. Apparently Carrageen is in Paris. Whether he went by Dublin or Cork, he had to pass the security men. And this is the quietest time of the year. Are there so many peers on the move that nobody noticed, or thought of it when the kidnapping story broke? And his car, you had the details of that. Why has nobody found it? It must be lying about at Dublin airport or near Cork harbour. Haven't you any Gardai there? It looks to me,' he concluded, gravely wagging his head, 'as if Marvell will have to write a follow-up about all that.'

His interrogator shifted uncomfortably in his chair.

Reresby's cool factual account of the police activities, their harrassing of rural dean, local doctor, butcher, postman, had entranced the public almost more than anything else: the last thing they would welcome was another such piece on what they had failed to do.

'What brought Mr Marvell here in the first place?' he asked, more politely.

'We were at Oxford together and he wanted to look me up.'

'And stay, to make extensive use of your phone and move in altogether. Well, I won't delay you. You know more than you're letting on but we'll leave it there for just now.'

'I suppose it was I who rang up Radio Eireann,' said Francis, looking hurt. 'I never knew I had a Bogside accent. And what about the subsequent demands from the Progs? Say the whole affair was a hoax – how did they know that Carrageen had slipped off to Paris at all?'

'If he had,' said the officer with a meaning look, and rose to leave. 'If you changed your mind, Mr Barraclough, you could give me a ring.' He wrote down his name and a telephone number and passed it across. 'Just a ring, now, don't say anything. I'd come round.'

'A nasty suspicious man, Inspector Drummond,' said Francis to Marigold, when the visitor had gone. 'I'm sure he half believes old Fishy is here, trussed up in the cellar.'

'Why doesn't he get on to the French police, and have them check the hotels?'

'It will not have occurred to him. He lives in a world of his own.'

But later on, with the beaming Reresby back from his errand and his lordship's card en route for the *Chronicle* office, his conscience pricked him a little. The rain had cleared and the sun shone out, and he decided to take a stroll to the village and have a word or two with Drummond, who had his headquarters there. As he came up to the barracks, Mr Quirke was just coming out, his face dark with unutterable things.

'Have you heard from Mr Maguire at all?' he asked, aggressively.

'Not exactly "heard from",' was the gay reply. 'Didn't you know I had kidnapped him too?'

Mr Quirke swept past him, muttering.

On hearing who the visitor was, Drummond gave orders for him to be admitted at once and for the two of them to be left alone. Francis was ushered into the bleak little room where the Sergeant had interviewed him: Drummond sat at the table with an expectant look on his face and a pile of foolscap before him.

'Going to make a clean breast of it after all?' he asked, in the fatherly way that police put on when criminals are prepared to talk, and holding his pen ready poised.

'Not really. I had a hunch that might help you. Did you ever trace that girl in the car, Rose O'Malley?'

The Guards had kept their patient but fruitless search to themselves.

'There's nothing in that,' Drummond said crossly, laying down his pen. 'There were a number of Rose O'Malleys in the area who corresponded to the particulars given, but all were sound, all at home, except for one in Retreat at the Visitation convent, Cork. Why?'

'Who told you the odd one was at the Visitation?'

'Her mother, of course, who else? The girl goes there three or four times a year, she's deeply religious.'

'And you didn't check with the convent?'

Drummond opened his mouth and shut it again, swallowing hard. Then he got up and strode from the room. Francis could hear him barking away, while the Sergeant got in a feeble moan here and there. Followed the sounds of a telephone call in which Drummond's voice, crisp and authoritative at first, grew steadily more and more apologetic until he seemed on the brink of tears. At last he returned, looking dazed and distracted.

'Nuns!' he said bitterly. 'That was Reverend Mother. Guards ringing up the Visitation. Never was known before. No, a Rose O'Malley was not with them and never had been. What ever next? She'd thank them to keep this out of the papers. And she's going to complain me to the bishop. Now what the devil,' he exploded, turning his own sense of failure, Irish style, to wrath against another, 'put this into your head?'

'Lord Carrageen is a bit of a card. He was dropping hints of a honeymoon that he meant to take. I imagine the girl in the car is the fortunate lady. All you need do now is, comb Paris for a crazy old man and a girl with scarlet hair.'

144

Well content with the result of his little démarche, Francis bade him a warm good evening and withdrew.

At the Castle, he found Colonel Beaulieu in full hunting kit, celebrating the good news with Marigold and Reresby. He had been out since early morning and only heard it, shouted by a lad on a bicycle, as he came trotting home. The hounds having killed thrice, he was in great trim already, and Carrageen's safety put the finishing touch to his happiness. He laughed over Reresby's despatch until the tears rolled down his cheeks, and he was full of admiration for the author.

'Clever young dogs, how you ferret things out!' he chortled. 'Mustn't ask how you did it, must I? Like asking the chef what he puts in the dinner. But this beats everything. Could only happen in Ireland! Those roadblocks – they'd do better in Abyssinia! And all the time that rascal Fishy...' He was obliged to break off, overcome.

But, even as they drank and made merry, storm clouds were gathering. The press corps were smarting under rebukes and queries from their employers and were putting their heads together. The Guards had assured them that, so far as they knew, there was no evidence of the story's truth. They were not saying, mind you, that Marvell had made it up, but they could see no way by which he had come by the facts. For their part, until confirmation was to hand, they must continue the search as if it had never been written.

Then, on the six o'clock news, came a further announcement from the Progs. The tale of Carrageen's being in Paris was a lie: he was in their custody and, if their demands were not met forthwith, would be executed without further delay. The Progressives' patience being exhausted, the time limit would not be extended again.

'A face-saver,' Francis observed. 'They'll keep mum from now on until it is all forgotten. Then after years and years, when Fishy is long since gathered, they'll revive the yarn of how their forbears once put paid to a hereditary foe of the Irish people, and it will become part of the national myth.'

The press corps thought otherwise, however. On the following day, the newspapers united in questioning the authenticity of Reresby's facts, quoting the official doubt, stressing that the hunt was still on and giving prominence to the Prog's ulti-

145

matum. The English made no editorial comment, but the Irish fumed over the irresponsibility of foreign journalists, who had so often damaged the country's name before. One, under the heading 'Stage Irish', asked piteously, if they ever would cease to look upon Ireland as a joke. 'An old and ailing man lies under the threat of murder,' it added: 'the whole country is on the alert, no stone has been left unturned, prayers have been offered in every church, and a frivolous chancer sweeps it under the carpet like any old soiled glove.'

Reresby was not in the least put out, in fact he greatly relished the concerted attack upon him. Lord Carrageen could not lie doggo in Paris forever, and when he bobbed up it would round the saga off nicely. But there was a factor in the case of which he was unaware.

The *Daily Chronicle* had once been a true-blue God-Crown-and-County journal of high repute and still profited by the afterglow of that era. But some years ago a curious individual had appeared with an itch for acquiring newspapers, any newspapers, regarding them as trophies rather than sources of fact and opinion. Indeed, he had no settled opinion himself, and no real policy. As long as the paper made money, it could take any political line that it chose. He bought the *Chronicle*, put in bright new editors and commanded them to get the paper out of the red; it now had taken to fashionable trends, scandal and what it called 'investigative journalism', and in plan language meant, poking around in murky corners. Unfettered by delicacy or scruple, it published whatever would make the loudest splash.

Thus, their natural reply to these press allegations was to publish a photograph of Lord Carrageen's card on page one. When the paper arrived on the Thursday evening, Reresby could hardly believe his eyes. Childhood in a country parsonage, schooling at Rugby and Magdalen, had not prepared him for these up-to-the-minute points of view.

'I never met such people before,' he said lamely. 'I never knew they existed.'

'You couldn't!' Francis consoled him. 'Some things one can imagine, others, one has to experience.'

'All I intended was, to show them the story was true. I shall resign, of course.'

146

'Sleep on that,' counselled his friend. 'From what I gather, anywhere else would be much the same.'

He spent a troubled evening himself, waiting for the reproaches of those he had kept in the dark; and when none came he assumed they had sent him to Coventry. He need not have worried about them, however, as the truth was completely different. When the rescue committee got home, all but Dr McLeod from the Hunt, he from his medical rounds, a card from Fishy awaited each one. These cards had been posted, like that to Francis, on Monday the 2nd November but, through chance or fanciful teamwork by the French and Irish mails, only delivered now. Their recipients were far too relieved by the outcome, too amused by the pictures, and too busy concealing them from their wives, to bother about the *Chronicle* or anything else; and their cup was filled when the Rector rang them one by one to say that Reresby was vindicated, as he had received that morning a most delightful card from their missing friend. This was of the Eiffel Tower, and gave a brief account of an imaginary trip to Versailles.

But there were all the others to whom no cards were sent and to whom the name of Francis Barraclough once more was anathema. These people were beside themselves with fury. The cur had known the facts all along and coldbloodedly laughed up his sleeve at the neighbours' distress. The old stories against him were raked up over again, the repudiation by his father for cowardice, the all-but-murder of that father by his engagement and the cynical wedding while the old man lay in his coffin, the attempt to cheat Maguire of his legacy and to make him look a fool when this proved impossible, the throwing of the family diamonds into a disused shaft – and the final outrage now. A chorus of hatred arose and hummed with mounting vigour all evening, fed by Miss Hackle, weakly endorsed by Miss Hilary Baggot on her bed of pain and swelled to a mighty volume by Mr Quirke, in whose opinion lynching for such a man was far too good.

And yet the very next day it all died down and never was heard again. The sudden dramatic change was due to events which passed into local legend as Barraclough's Ride. They will be recorded, accurately for the first and last time, in the pages that follow.

# Chapter Nineteen

'I suspect that you are in pig,' Francis said to Marigold across the breakfast table next morning. Reresby was sound asleep in Blenheim, worn out by the excitements of the day before.

'You do have an elegant style of talk,' she replied, her dimples appearing. 'I believe so too, but I wanted to be sure. How did you guess? It can't show yet.'

'Oh, that sort of greyhound look in the face that women get.'

'Your eyes are as sharp as your tongue,' she said happily: this observation on his part gave her a nice warm wrapped-up feeling. 'We'll see. Why are you in your riding outfit?'

'A gallop over the sands will do me good. And I want to think.'

'Shall I come along?'

'No. I tell you, I want to think.'

'And you can't, when I'm by?'

'Whoever could?' he asked, blowing a kiss.

'You might anyways tell me what to do about Mrs Jeffars. She's been here nearly a week – oughtn't she to have wages? And I was trying to get her to say what she planned to do when Maguire came back. All the expression went out of her voice, and she answered, maybe he wouldn't be coming at all.'

'That is certainly odd,' Francis remarked. 'The "maybe he wouldn't" sounds like a hint that she knows he will not. It is only when they know nothing that they come out with positive statements. And yet, Maguire and she were hardly on letter-writing terms. Don't worry about the wages, though. She likes it here, and we'll give her a present when she leaves. Now I'm off, before the tide starts turning. Here, Juno!'

The estate was bounded to the north by a long lane with tall fuchsia hedges on either side, leading down to the strand. When the tide was out, the Reef stood up like a row of huge wicked fangs, the ruined hulk balanced awkwardly across them. Behind that was a stretch of sand, good and firm for a

148

gallop, worse than concrete for a fall. As Francis turned off the road into the lane, he noticed that a vehicle had been driving up and down it. The rain had softened the earth and there were many deep tracks overlaying each other. Hardly tourists, he thought, at this time of year. It must be men from the estate, fetching loads of sand for building they had to do. They always got this from the shore, well knowing that salty sea-sand held the damp and made it useless. There was clean dry sand in a local quarry, but that was some distance away and called for extra effort in the collecting. It also made for added work when the walls they put up came tumbling down, but this they appeared unable to grasp. They were like those Russian peasants in *Anna Karenin* that Levin had to struggle with, he reflected; not a penny to choose between them.

But when he reached the top of the lane, he found a car drawn up to one side under the protective leafy fuchsias, and he was more annoyed than ever. He loathed this beastly habit of dumping vehicles no longer required and leaving them dotted about to rust away. This did not look like a crock, how-ever, it was a new Marina for all the inevitable dents and scratches. And it could not belong to a local man, having number plates from another part of the country, he vaguely thought from the North. Another thing – write-offs were left any old how, whereas this had been carefully turned with bonnet towards the road, ready for use again.

He reined in and leant forward to examine it better. There was one of those foolish toys, a spotted dog, fixed in the back window to dance about and irritate drivers behind, and a statue of St Christopher beside the steering wheel. It must belong to a holidaymaker after all, for there was a suitcase on the floor at the back. But then he observed that this was made of excellent quality leather, not at all the cheap fibre job secured with string that went with the dog and the statue. There was something familiar about its appearance too. Peeping through the window, he saw the initials on the case, A.G.B. A.G.B. His father's initials. He realized with a nasty shock that this was his father's case and this, Maguire's car. The dents and scratches were those inflicted by Lord Carrageen on the Limerick road. Maguire had never gone to England at all. What could have

149

happened? Where had he gone?

Well, that put paid to the gallop. The quickest way to Ballinaween and the Guards was by skirting the foreshore back to the Castle and thence by the river down to the road. He urged his horse on and broke into a canter along the grassy verge. When they had passed the hulk, he turned his head to make sure that Juno was following; but she had halted in her tracks and, rigid, was pointing the hulk like a gun-dog, one paw raised, nose and tail-tip in a dead straight line. He shouted to her, but she took no notice. Creeping a few yards nearer, she pointed again and, all at once with a howl, dashed forward and leaped over the side, vanishing into the hold.

Next came a confused shouting, and three short men, whose shaggy hair and grubby waterproofs proclaimed them heroes of the resistance, hove into sight on the deck and jumped overboard, picking themselves up and making tracks for the car. Their one thought, it was clear, was to escape from the ravening hellhound that had disturbed them: their terror was marvellous to see. Francis called on them to stop. One of them did so, drawing a revolver and firing two shots in his direction, before scampering after the others. He heard the dull phut! phut! of the bullets passing his head, and then the Marina started and raced away.

Juno was still down in the hulk, rending the air with her agonized cries. He leaped from his horse and flew to the rescue, imagining they might have taken a crowbar to her. But she was unharmed, flinging herself with all her might again and again at the closed door of a cabin. He scrambled down the companion-way and kicked in the door, to be sent flying as Juno tore past him to get in ahead.

There was Maguire, tied hand and foot, with sticking plasters over his mouth, pale, haggard and wild-eyed. Francis gently pulled the plasters away and seized a knife that lay on the floor to cut the ropes, while Juno ecstatically licked the prisoner's face, hands and any part of him that he could get at.

'Thank Gawd, Mr Francis!' gasped the unfortunate man. 'They was going to do me. Only waiting on the tide. They was for putting a stone round me neck, and heaving me in.'

'Shut up,' said Francis. 'We have to get you out of this.'

150

He dragged Maguire, who could hardly stand, let alone walk, up the steps to the rotting deck and over the gunwale. 'Get on my back,' he said then, bending over as if for a game of leapfrog, and tottered with his burden to where his mount was placidly munching grass. 'Hopla!' He hoisted him with a prodigious effort on the animal's back and sprang into the saddle himself. 'Hold on tight. I'm going as fast as Shreddie will.'

All this time he had merely been acting, hardly thinking at all. Only when they were safe at the Castle, Maguire in bed, Juno crouched alongside, her huge lavender eyes fixed lovingly on him, Dr McLeod on his way and an urgent call to Inspector Drummond put in, did the pieces of this grotesque puzzle begin to fit together. It was unbelievable. The clowns had done it again. They had come to nab Lord Carrageen, blundered up to the wrong address and made away with Maguire. In their fathomless stupidity, they could see no difference between a decrepit country gentleman and a sturdy man of the people.

'I told 'em,' croaked Maguire, reviving fast in the warmth of Marigold's tender concern and lavish helpings of Scotch. 'They wouldn't believe me. They said, where did I get me posh English accent, then?' A flicker of gratification showed in the care-lined face at the thought. 'And they were going to do me today, when the Government didn't release them showers in gaol. And they would of, only for you, Mr Francis.'

'Only for Juno.' The idea of those vermin, all set to drown a defenceless man, fleeing in panic from that dearest, most lamblike, of creatures, was a very agreeable one.

Dr MacLeod prescribed complete rest, plenty of nourishing food and an easy hand with the Scotch. 'They haven't injured him, but it has been a terrible strain. Seems they told him it was all for Ireland, as if that were a consolation. If he goes into shock, call me at once,' he said to Marigold, who had taken charge of the sickroom. 'Good lad, Francis,' he said on his way out. 'You're Arthur's son, all right.'

'It was Juno,' Francis repeated.

An hour or so later, Inspector Drummond arrived. His face had shed the wintry aspect it had worn at their previous discussions, and like the doctor he had pleasant things to say. 'Smart

151

of you to note the registration and remember the spotted dog, Mr Barraclough. They must have put it up to look like commercial travellers, and it only helped to give 'em away. We've got 'em, all wanted men. Now I must trouble you for a statement, and Maguire too, if he's able.'

'Could you keep this quiet for a bit?' Francis asked. 'It's another fine break for Marvell.'

The Inspector looked at him gravely. 'You and your postcard,' he said. 'Wanted to con me, did you, there was a crystal ball behind it? We'll have to announce the arrests, the Minister is losing his mind. But we could stretch a point with Maguire. He was never reported missing.'

When they reached the part that Juno had played in the rescue, Drummond lay back in his chair and burst out laughing. 'We need a dog like that in the Force!'

'Oh, she wasn't after the men,' Francis explained. 'That old hulk wasn't hers. She had scented Maguire, if "scented" is the word, poor chap.'

The Inspector shuddered. 'Begod, yes. Some of our lads were round at that wreck. 'Twould have sickened a hog, they say.'

'Now may I give the story to Marvell?' asked Francis, when the statement was complete and signed.

'You may, of course. And thanks very much.'

Reresby was still fast asleep, and growled crossly when Francis shook him. On hearing the reason for it, however, he tumbled out of bed and got to work at once. Presently the wire to London was humming again.

Marigold was in the drawing-room, curled up on a sofa. 'Maguire is sleeping like the dead,' she told her husband. 'Guess the Inspector finished him off. For pity's sake, I never heard tell of such doings in all my days.'

'No? Not even with the coloured people at home?' he teased her, sinking down and putting an arm round her waist. 'I did. There was the time they went to blow up the top brass of the paras at Aldershot. They bagged five waitresses, a gardener and a Catholic padre. It's in the great tradition.'

He said nothing to her about the revolver shots, which mercifully had been aimed at him. Had they been fired at random, most likely he would be dead by now, and Marigold left to wait for their baby alone.

'It's just too terrible, kind of creepy,' Marigold said, nestling up to him. 'Maguire came down with his case and got into the car, and the three were waiting there before him. He gave a holler or two before he was gagged, but we were busy with the Hallowe'en party. Playing at bob-apple and lucky dip! What sort of goddam place is this?'

'Just Ireland,' Francis replied, with the experience of four hundred years.

'And Mrs Jeffars has gone, vamoosed. Do you think she knew?'

'Might have. If she did, we shall never find out.'

The Inspector was true to his word and yet, in some mysterious way, the story spread about. Shortly afterwards everyone in the village, except the press corps, knew it: how Francis, guided by intuition, had gone to look at the hulk in the Reef: how he found half a dozen dangerous men there, armed to the teeth: how, single-handed and unarmed, he stormed it, seized their weapons and took them prisoner: how he had found his supplanter Maguire, apparently dead, and brought him back with the kiss of life: how he then galloped off with the inert body slung over the horse's neck – 'for all the world,' as one erudite character put it, 'like the rape of the Sabine women.'

This was a plain, unvarnished account, off the cuff: embellishments were added later.

Last thing that night, before he turned in, Francis went to have a look at the invalid. He found him broad awake, staring pensively at the ceiling, and washed as clean as a baby. Marigold in her kindness had offered to give him a bed-bath, and his shame and horror at the suggestion had forced him, groggy as he was, to get up and attend to the matter himself.

'Well, Maguire, those men are in quod and anyhow, the Guards are keeping watch,' he said. 'Now relax and forget all about it. You are safe, back in your own house again.'

'Mr Francis, no,' replied Maguire. 'I've bin thinking. I've had it. I'm not cut out for this lark, even without them showers, takin' me for a lord and tryin' to do me. I wanted to be a swell, right, always did, even as a nipper. Saw what other people

153

had and thought, why can't I have the same? But there's more to it than I knew. Honest to God, I haven't had me peace of mind since the Major died. And, funny thing, I never felt like I was nothing, not when he was there. It was afterwards, when I was reely meant to be someone. No, soon as I'm on me legs, I'm sugarin' off to London.'

'It's natural you should feel that now,' said Francis. 'But you must take your time and think it over. My father left you this place. He would not have done so if he thought you unfit.'

'He left me the place because I saved his life, didden he?' asked Maguire. ''Scuse me bringin' it up. And now you've been and saved mine. We're quits, and no more about it.' He closed his eyes with a contented sigh, but re-opened them almost at once. 'Of course, Mr Francis, if you cared to top up me pension, I wouldn't say no.'

Nothing that Francis could say would induce him to change his mind.

'Tell that Mr Goodchild to get weaving at once, with whatever. And that's me final word.' Turning on his side with a dismissive air, he composed himself to slumber again.

'It seems we're stuck here, darling, after all,' Francis said to Marigold, climbing into bed beside her. 'Maguire has thrown in his hand.'

'Well, there are worse places to be, Progs or no Progs,' she said drowsily. 'And this is where you belong. I knew that right bang off, the minute we got here and you started moaning about it all. And the way you bossed them all around. In the Quai Voltaire, you were scared of the concierge, and smoking like a chimney with nerves. Paris – that was just fighting with Daddy.'

From the kennels came a murmur, as if of approval, a little tentative yowling, some practice arpeggios; and then, finding their voices, the pack lifted them up and melodiously greeted the moon.

'And I sure would have missed those dogs,' Marigold mumbled, her own voice trailing away.

'Hounds, darling,' said Francis mechanically, halfway through a prodigious yawn.

In another minute or two, the pair were soundly sleeping.

154

# Chapter Twenty

It was rare for Mr Goodchild to read anything in the *Chronicle* apart from the deaths and obituaries. Many of his senior clients took it because they had always done so, and he, merely to keep abreast of their demises. It was still more rare, indeed almost unknown, for him to laugh aloud; but on this one occasion he did both things together.

He was in high good humour already, being engaged on a task that was much to his liking and one that he had never dared to hope for: namely he was drafting a preliminary document *in re* Castle Reef and the transfer of its ownership. When Mr Twigg came in with the newspaper, folded back, and an item heavily marked with blue pencil, he greeted him with a benevolent smile.

'Excuse me for interrupting you, Mr Goodchild,' the junior partner said, trying to keep his voice steady. 'But Morrow and I thought you would wish to know of this without delay.'

Under the headline 'Stage Irishry Again', the feature ran:

This journal has been accused of treating Ireland in a light and irreverent fashion, and of drawing a long bow in our descriptions of it. Nothing has been further from our minds; but, to clear ourselves of the charge, we print below, verbatim and without any comment, a letter we have received from a Mr Aloysius Quirke, solicitor, of Ballinaween, the village where happened those recent stirring events reported exclusively by us. We have not presumed to make any changes in Mr Quirke's manner of presentation: the letter runs, 'Dear Sirs, In your issue of 13th instant you published the photograph of a postcard from my Client, Lord Carrageen, addressed to Mr Francis Barraclough, both resident in this locality. My Client wrote from Paris, where he is on Holidays, and the wording of that postcard meant, or could mean, or might be taken by reasonable parsons as meaning,

155

that he was engaged in dubious or amorous activities there. Such imputations on a man, of my Client's standing is highly defamatory, suggesting that he was a man of low morals and infamous character, and in generally holding him up to hatred, ridicule and contempt. He is still abroad, but has granted me full powers to manage his legal affairs while away. It is to be hoped that this matter may be settled promptly, for which our terms would be: a full apology from yourselves, to be given the same Prominence, as the photograph had, and the payment of a solatium appropriate to the scale of the damage sustained, with all legal costs and expenses: failing which, I shall have no alternative but to begin, Proceedings without further notice. Yours faithfully, Aloysius Benedict Quirke.

Mr Goodchild had received the paper from Twigg with an air of courteous interest; but as he read it, his face took on an expression of incredulity, turning to stupefaction, until he finally passed it back with something near a guffaw.

'Dear me,' he crowed, with shaking sides. 'I had the pleasure of meeting that gentleman. And it is he who is pestering us about the Barraclough jewels, if you remember. I trust this will come on in the High Court. A pretty little case, very pretty indeed. And a fitting curtain to the whole mad story.

'And that reminds me, Twigg,' he said, pulling himself together and solemnly tapping the draft on his desk, 'of something which cannot be said too often and which you and Morrow should earnestly impress on all your clients. A man with property to bequeath should always make his Will bearing in mind that he may be dead tomorrow. No good has ever come, nor will it ever come, of attempting to arrange affairs with an eye to the distant future.'